MENDING WALLS
with the billionaire

OTHER BOOKS BY LORIN GRACE

MENDING WALLS
with the billionaire

LORIN GRACE

CURRANT
CREEK PRESS

Cover Design © 2018 LJP Creative
Photos © Deposit Photos, back cover photo curtesy of Serventures.com

Formatting by LJP Creative
Edits by Eschler Editing

Published by Currant Creek Press
North Logan, Utah

Mending Walls with the Billionaire © 2018 by Lorin Grace

First edition: September 2018
ISBN: 978-0-9984110-8-8

For Evan
THE BEST BIG BROTHER I NEVER HAD.

one

DEAH EVANS PATTED ARACELI'S HAND. "What caught your attention during the presentation tonight?"

Araceli searched for the right words to describe her feelings to the wife of her father's best friend, but the impression left by the slides of Haitian orphans rendered verbal explanation inadequate. "The face of the girl in the brown pillow-case dress—it's like she wants to hide but be noticed at the same time. She is me when I was her age. I want to tell her I understand."

"Ah, that's my Miss Tia. Most people choose the younger children. You read her emotion correctly. I can't talk about her specific background, but as I explained, some of our children have come out of human-trafficking situations or other orphanages the government shut down because they exploited the children while the owners pocketed the money."

"Why hasn't she been adopted?"

"Tia turned fourteen last fall. There is no hope for adoption because the process is so complicated. She would age out before the final paperwork is complete. Children like Tia need the interaction they receive from these service trips to help them see their future can be more than their past."

"Can a weeklong visit do that?"

"The service weeks give the children an opportunity to learn skills they can't learn in school and to experience new ideas. I believe seeing women who are going to college helps the teenage girls see the value of education. Most won't have the means to get further education without a sponsor or scholarships, but they need to build the desire and a thirst for more. We worry about sponsors later."

"So why the summer family-group trips?"

"The family unit as we know it is a foreign concept to many Haitians. Family groups teach by example what a class never will. At the Evans Foundation, we feel building stronger families builds a stronger Haiti. More than a third of the children at the orphanage have known-parents living in Haiti."

"So they are not really orphans?"

"No, their parents believe the lie that the orphanages can do a better job raising their children." Deah turned to her husband, who joined them and took his hand.

"After seeing this, I need to go on one of the service trips." Araceli didn't mention the money factor. The last of her savings had paid for her final semester at school. With a younger sister in college, too, Dad would not hand out a loan or gift. Compelled. She hadn't felt that about anything for years.

Frank Evans put his arm around his wife. "According to your dad, your spring break is the same time as the Dallas-area universities' break. You should join us. We don't often make service trips composed of college students. Our summer trips are mostly high school students and families. Kyle leads those."

Kyle? She'd tried not to think of him their entire visit. Knowing he guided the other trips made the spring-break trip her only option.

Mrs. Evans looped her arm through her husband's. "For the spring-break trip, I ask that participants create their own projects, some of which will be continued in the summer and fall trips. You will need to submit a proposal for a project. Even those who end up working on other projects are asked to do so. Sometimes we find the timing isn't right but the idea is solid. I have seen some of your paintings. Think about how you can incorporate that talent."

Araceli's mother, Terri, joined them. "Rich says it is starting to snow. He wants to get home before it accumulates on Mass Pike."

Deah smiled at her husband. "We'd better get back to our hotel. Frank knows I would talk about Haiti all night if I could. I've heard about how fast your Boston blizzards can accumulate, and we could be stuck here until spring."

"But Deah would finally have enough time to talk about her work." Frank laughed as he ushered his wife away.

Araceli followed her parents out to their car. "Mom, I want to go to Haiti."

"I hear that, but how are you going to come up with the money? Our circumstances haven't changed, and with both you and Amelia in college, there isn't any extra for a volunteer trip."

"I can get a part-time job on campus. Early morning cus-todial jobs are always open. There is something ironic about cleaning bathrooms to pay to go to a country with questionable plumbing."

Terri raised her eyebrows but didn't comment, her doubts radiating like the heater in the old Ford Dad drove. But the eyes of all the children, not just the girl Mrs. Evans had called Miss Tia, called to Araceli begging her to come.

One way or another, she was going to Haiti.

"Marci, hurry up!" Kyle Evans yelled up the stairs.

Marci came out of the bathroom and leaned over the banister. "Why? You're not going anywhere tonight. It's lame to pretend you're sick on New Year's."

"I am not pretending." Kyle coughed for emphasis.

"You could at least do like Cassie and claim you have to work tonight." Marci checked her lipstick in the mirror. "Even Mark found a date."

Marci tossed Kyle the keys. "Come on. I still don't see why you have to drive me."

"Mom and Dad are worried about you driving home after midnight, and remember…"

"I know, I know. Text X if anything feels wrong."

Kyle resisted the urge to muss his youngest sister's hair. "Are we giving EmilyAnne a ride?"

"Her dad will pick us up on the way home from the party he is going to. Even old people are going out and having fun. You need to get a life."

"And you need to get in the truck before you drive me crazy." Kyle held open the door.

After dropping his sister off, Kyle returned to his parents' place. He preferred to sleep at his own condo, but he'd promised to keep tabs on Marci while Mom and Dad were in Boston. Both his other siblings had plans tonight. Cassie claimed she needed to be on hand at the hospital for the New Year's baby and subsequent announcement. And Mark appeared to be determined to spend as much of his holiday as he could playing before returning to MIT. If Kyle hadn't found an empty cereal box in the middle of the table each morning, he would doubt the existence of his brother.

Perhaps Kyle shouldn't have used his little cold as an excuse to skip the parties tonight, but he wasn't into watching people consume more alcohol than they could handle or women hitting on him because they'd seen an article on his grandfather in Dallas Magazine and had spotted him in the photo on the third page. The last two women he'd dated were more interested in his bank account than he was. He hadn't done anything to earn his fortune. And preparing to take over the charitable arm of his grandfather's corporation meant he was only good at spending the family fortune wisely.

His grandfather had always encouraged his children and grandchildren to find their own paths and careers. Kyle had studied family therapy, while Cassie trained to be an RN, then earned an MBA. Some of his cousins chose law and accounting and planned to take their place in the family business. Mark had studied chemistry, thinking someday he might revolutionize Grandfather's oil company. Kyle would eventually take his mother's role as the chairman of philanthropic outreach, but for now he only wanted to focus on one thing—Haiti.

He had fallen in love at first sight—with both the country and the orphanage his family helped support. He loved the 120 orphans who didn't care how many zeros came before the decimal in his bank account as long as he could throw a solid curveball.

Twice he took women on service trips to Haiti because he hoped they might be the elusive one. Wrong. The second had flown back to the States after only two days. The first refused to leave the airport. The only woman who'd stuck it out was Cassie's friend Jade. The problem was that after a slew of dates, there was zero chemistry, and Jade couldn't take no to mean no. He was sure Jade kept signing up for the service tours to impress him because she didn't seem to connect with the Haitians.

As a cheer rose from the television and the ball dropped, Kyle made a resolution—find a woman who loved Haiti more than she loved his money.

two

THE GROUP CHAT WAS FULL of ideas for projects for the Haitian orphanage. Araceli couldn't help but feel left out, as most of the volunteers for the spring-break trip were from Dallas and often abandoned the chat room to get coffee. As the only volunteer from Indiana, she didn't know anyone other than Deah Evans and her husband. Not that she really knew them, either—they were friends of her parents. Before last Christmas, she'd only met them one other time when she was ten and the family visited. Their children were near the same ages, and they'd had a lot of fun—until their oldest son had proven downright mean.

Araceli turned her attention back to the ideas being tossed about in the forum. One of the women was a fashion-design major who proposed teaching the interested orphans basic sewing skills and helping them make their own clothing. Of all the ideas presented, Araceli liked the sewing class the best, but she didn't sew. Deah had asked each of them to come up with an idea, but Araceli was stumped. The guys in construction management and civil engineering would help with the previously planned project of weatherizing the roof, but she couldn't do that. She didn't garden. She didn't have nursing qualifications. How could she make a difference?

The hum of the garage door opening echoed throughout the house. Not wanting her roommates to see her frustration, Araceli closed the chat program and brought up the essay for English on her computer screen. The last nonart class on her schedule. Hallelujah.

As car doors slammed and laughter carried into the house, Araceli hastily typed the next line. Just as she finished, the door connecting to the kitchen opened, and Candace walked in carrying a bag of groceries, the green plastic sack almost perfectly matching the color of her spiky hair.

"Araceli can have the deciding vote." Candace dropped the bag on the counter.

"Deciding vote on what?" Araceli closed the laptop and moved it off the table before Candace's cousin Zoe set a couple of pizza boxes on the table.

Zoe opened the first box and swiped the pepper from the top. "The Friday Night Art Society project this semester. I think we should paint the history of women artists, including illustrators and graphic designers, in the stairwell going down to the laundry room."

Candace shuddered. "I told Zoe that as the newest member of the house, she only gets a half vote."

"So it balances out Tessa's vote since she is only here part of the semester?" Araceli wanted out of the vote. For the first time in four years, she didn't care what the project of the semester would be. Realizing halfway through her senior year that she'd made a mistake in her choice of major had left her feeling trapped. Art was useless.

"I hadn't considered Tessa's vote. The way she has been the past three weeks, she might request cupids on the ceiling of Lover's Loft, as she is up there on the phone every free minute she's got." Candace set six plates on the table.

"Who else is coming?" Araceli peeked inside the other pizza box. Canadian bacon and pineapple. "Mandy?"

Candace closed the lid before Araceli could snatch a piece.

"She should be here with Abbie any minute. Daniel went to Japan for the week."

"Who is Abbie?" Zoe set the cups on the table.

Araceli pulled some baby spinach out of the fridge to make a salad. "Abbie is part of Daniel's security team."

The front door slammed. "Hey, guys." Tessa waved and turned down the hallway to her room.

"Hurry back! Pizza's getting cold." Candace tossed some tomatoes into the salad.

The doorbell rang. Before Zoe could answer, a man entered, followed by two women. Araceli put a hand over her mouth to keep from laughing at Zoe's reaction to Mr. Alexander. Mandy's bodyguard was the type of man that made most women forget to breathe and invaded a daydream or two. If he ever wanted to do side work as a cover model for romance novels, they wouldn't need to manipulate his photos.

Candace barely acknowledged the bodyguard's presence as she pulled her former roommate into a hug.

Zoe closed her mouth and came over to Araceli and whispered, "Who is he?"

"Mr. Alexander. Abbie's twin. Word of caution—don't call him Alex unless he gives you permission. He says the title keeps him professional."

After checking all the windows, Mr. Alexander exited, and the other women came into the kitchen.

Having changed into a pair of jeans and T-shirt, Tessa joined the group by the door. Mandy looped her arm through Candace's. "I am so sorry about this, but Daniel has gone a bit overboard. It wasn't even a threatening Tweet."

Candace turned to Abbie. "Glad I didn't remove the cameras. Abbie, do you get to eat with us, or are you on duty too?"

"I'm on duty, but I have the easier of the duties because my job is to be one of the crowd, at least until you start painting." Abbie took a seat in the corner.

Candace rapped a spoon on the table. "Ladies, we're a couple weeks late, but welcome to the first meeting of the Friday Night Art Society this year. In honor of January, the dessert is ice cream."

Mandy laughed. "The desert is always ice cream. This time I am adding pickles."

Tessa was the first to scream. "Really??"

"Can I be Aunt Candace?"

Araceli clapped her hands. "Hence the extra bodyguards?"

Mandy smiled at Abbie. "Yes, Daniel has them babysitting six months early. Poor Abbie gets the brunt of it. I've already offered her a month's extra vacation when the baby arrives. Seriously, who wants to guard a woman with morning sickness?"

Candace took a piece of the veggie pizza. "I know! This semester's project can be the nursery at the cottage!" The home Daniel rebuilt for Mandy before their engagement was their regular weekend getaway from Chicago.

There was no need for a vote.

Putting off reviewing grant applications never worked out. The last Friday night in January found Kyle staring at his computer screen. Once the review team vetted the requests, his assistant organized applications by type, need, and her own sincerity scale. Occasionally she added links to social media or news stories, primarily on the applications she considered less than worthy. Her you-should-fund-this-project pile was thoroughly researched and often included extra tidbits and personal stories.

At his grandfather's request, Kyle needed to personally review every application. Perhaps fifty years ago, when Grandfather had implemented the policy of gifting 10 percent of the corporation's profits, it was feasible to review every application, but the applications had more than doubled each year since Kyle had inherited the responsibility once belonging to his mother.

One set of applications was marked with a new label: "Highly Unusual." Kyle studied the forms before reaching for his phone and calling his mother.

Deah didn't even bother with a hello. "You waited until the end of the month again, didn't you. Which application is perplexing you this time?"

Mildly affronted, Kyle laughed tightly. "Am I really so predictable?"

"I didn't think you were calling on a Friday night to tell me you met the woman of your dreams. If you were on a date, you wouldn't call me. I, however, am on a date with the man of my dreams, so do you mind if we hurry this up?"

The sound of his father's laughter echoed in the background. "Don't worry, we are still driving, but I'd say you get about ten minutes."

The joys of speakerphone.

"I have seventy-four applications from orphanages and schools in Haiti. Do you know what is going on? Has there been a policy change?"

"No, but a couple of the board members for the orphanage were there in November. They may have said the wrong thing to the wrong person. I hate how some Haitians see the orphans as a means to lining their pockets. No new projects in Haiti without a complete investigation. If any of the applications stand out, you could come with us on the spring-break service trip and do some detective work."

"Nice try. As much as I love Haiti, I am not going on this trip. Besides, I am going in three weeks to check on the progress of our last group of new orphans who came in after the raid on the traffickers. One of the girls was in their system for more than three years, and she isn't adjusting well. We may need to find a different situation for her."

"I saw the report. I want to create a halfway house of sorts—more of a home situation for children struggling to break the chains of slavery."

Kyle twirled his pen and pushed back from the desk. "It's a grand idea, but we are already having issues with staffing, and the house would need a professional therapist on staff. I'd need a month down there to find qualified employees."

"I still think you should come the end of March. Jade is a nice girl. She shouldn't prevent you from going. Not many Westlake girls can survive one of our trips for a day, and this is her third trip."

Kyle rolled his eyes. "Back to the applications. There's only one application for aid that looks worth investigating. It is for a little school run mostly by the mothers of the students. I can add a visit to my list for next trip. They are only asking for a couple hundred dollars so they can get more chickens and build a better fence."

"Oh, yes, one of the board members is quite fond of that little school. She calls them her queen bees because they work so hard. This is the first time they have applied for help."

"So, you are saying these mothers are doing what we have been advocating and coming up with their own solutions?"

"I think so. I'll forward a couple of emails to you about them. And—"

Kyle's father interrupted. "We are now at the Meyerson, so you are now on my date time. Y'all can hash this out later. And, Kyle, you don't need to work all the time. Have a good night."

The call disconnected, the ensuing silence mirroring that of the empty office.

After dinner, everyone went to the studio to sketch out their ideas. Mandy pulled Araceli into the library. "What is going on? You seem a bit down."

"I don't know. I look at finishing my BFA project and think what's the point? Art can't save the world. I chose a useless major." All graduating did was add another starving artist to the world.

"I know how frustrated I was finishing up my MFA last year. And you have had a couple of delays with your graduation. It didn't help that you had to move back to Massachusetts last year when you were sick. But artists *can* do good in the world. Grandma Mae said that a person doesn't need to change the whole world, just the world around them by being kind." Mandy sat on the couch and motioned for Araceli to join her.

"I know. But I want to make a difference in the world." Araceli knew she was pouting. For the past year it seemed like she would never graduate with her BFA when most of her roommates had completed their master's. Getting mono hadn't been part of her college plans, but she'd never regretted taking the semester off to go to Paris—even though the trip put her behind.

"You can make an impact with art. Have you considered helping with the art-therapy class over at the community center? My grandmother loved learning watercolor when I lived with her. You could switch to a BA and graduate now. Having any degree opens doors in other fields. Don't tell Tessa or Candace, but the *F* in the middle of BFA stands for 'fine,' and there are a lot of ways to be fine without the word on your diploma."

Stunned, Araceli didn't answer for a moment. "You are saying this after all your hard work?"

"My crowning glory was turning the Crawford Mansion into a house of ill repute. The freelance jobs I've taken will all be round filed in five years." Mandy moved her hand to her middle. "Now I am embarking on a different path. I am looking forward to motherhood. Believe me, BFA/MFA is not the be-all and end-all. In your case, art therapy may be much more fulfilling."

Araceli was one of the few to have seen the before version of the *Bordello de Crawford* photo manipulation Mandy had created to get over her crush on her now-husband.

"I hadn't thought of art therapy. I guess that would be making a difference in the world." Araceli pulled out her phone and did a quick search. "It looks like I would need a master's degree and to pick up some psych classes. I can look into it more." She didn't know how to express what she was feeling.

"Does this have anything to do with going to Haiti over spring break?"

"Listening to the Evans speak about their work in the orphanage and the school—they are changing lives!"

"How did you meet them?"

"Mr. Evans is an old college friend of my dad's. His wife is the daughter of a Texas oil magnate. But they don't seem like billionaires—no security team or anything like that. She reminds me of you. She runs the Evans Foundation on her own."

Mandy pulled out her phone. "Daniel has donated to a couple of foundations who work in Haiti. I wonder if they are one of them. He tries to be very careful as some of the orphanages there are less than reputable."

"That's what Deah says."

"Tessa said you were working early morning custodial to earn money for the trip."

Araceli stuck out her tongue. "There has to be some type of irony in cleaning toilets to earn money to go to a place where you can't flush toilet paper."

The blood drained from Mandy's face. "Ew, don't even make me think about that. How are you doing on earning the money you need to go?"

"If I am careful, I should be able to have the money. I am hoping the airline tickets don't go up before I can buy them." Paying for the trip equaling nearly half the semester's tuition was stretching her to the limit. But Foundation resources were not for volunteers.

"I have a proposition for you. How about I pay your airfare and lodging, and in return you provide Daniel and me a report on what Haiti is really like and what you feel could be done to improve things as well as on what is already working well."

Araceli bit her lip. The offer was so tempting. But her father had clearly stated that if she wanted to do this, it should be her sacrifice. "I couldn't take Daniel's money."

"Technically it isn't his. I have been doing some freelancing."

"Isn't that the same thing?"

"Not really. I have a huge household budget and an absolutely ridiculous clothing budget I never come close to spending. Daniel is frugal in many ways but not when it comes to me. So the money is all mine, and I don't have a thing to spend it on." Mandy tapped her abdomen. "Daniel went a bit crazy and gave me an insane budget for this little one. I am trying to convince him he doesn't need to spend so much on things. Sometimes Walmart works just as well. Now he is talking houses, and if I am not careful, he will build something as big as his grandfather's mansion-turned-community center."

"Wow, such a first-world problem." Araceli wasn't sure she could laugh until Mandy did.

"No, it is so much worse than a first-world problem. A first-world problem is forgetting to charge your cell phone. I don't even have a name for the types of problems billions of dollars cause. I want our children to be normal, and a full-detail security team for a pregnancy isn't normal."

"Do you still get threats?"

Mandy frowned. "One or two. There are some delusional and jealous women out there."

Araceli put an arm around her friend. "Death threats aren't normal either."

Abbie came around the corner. "Death threats?"

Mandy blew out a puff of air and shook her head. "Nothing new, Abbie."

"Well then, I suggest you get in the studio before Candace and Zoe come to blows. Those two fight worse than sisters. You'd think cousins would get along."

Araceli tucked her phone in her pocket. "Don't let them fool you. They love each other, but Zoe is a graphic designer. They would fight anyway."

three

PASSPORT NUMBER? ARACELI DUG THROUGH her drawer in search of the blue book. It would be helpful to be a bit more organized. But then, organization was overrated. Zoe's insistence that the mismatched plates and bowls be stacked in ROYGBIV order was a bit annoying. Only an artist would ever arrange dishes according to the colors of the rainbow. Candace had started wearing her wigs in reverse rainbow just to protest.

Araceli found the document in the second drawer. After entering the information and hitting Purchase, she leaned down to put the passport back in the drawer. No, it would get lost there. She should put it someplace she would be able to find it before the trip. Araceli dug through her closet. The fanny pack she'd taken to Paris would be perfect for Haiti. She finally located the little bag inside her large suitcase.

The money Mandy gave her would cover most of the cost of food and transportation. The best part would come Monday morning when she gave her two weeks' notice. Haiti was really happening.

Even getting her tetanus immunization updated and a typhoid shot sounded exciting.

Waiting seven more weeks was going to be the hard part.

Araceli sent off an email to Deah Evans with her flight confirmation numbers. There was no way she could concentrate on the English paper. She opened up the college website to see if she could switch majors three weeks into her final semester. Dad was going to be happy—the semester in Paris and the French literature class made graduating in May possible with dropping the BFA-project class. It also saved her money in supplies.

Araceli turned up her music and danced around the room. No project!

When the song ended, she emailed the academic advisor for her major, then called her mom.

"What do you think of this idea?" Deah Evans handed her son her tablet which was opened to her inbox.

Kyle read the letter. "Doing the handprint tree mural two years ago was fun for the children, and I agree more color would give the place a homier feel."

"But?"

"There is so much to be done that decorating seems like a waste of resources. I will admit I'm intrigued by her idea of using the styles of Haitian artists. The tree mural looks so American."

Deah took her tablet back. "What I would like to see is the children incorporated in this. One of the ideas behind the old handprint tree was to involve the children. I'll write her back and see if she has any ideas to help the children be part of this."

Kyle sat on the couch opposite his mom. "How many volunteers do you have for this trip?"

"Ten, including Marci's friend EmilyAnne, plus your father and me. You are sure you don't want to come?" Deah's smile indicated her awareness of his answer.

"No way. Jade has her sorority involved in this. The last two trips with her were enough to make me vow to never be near her again."

"She is a nice girl. Just not for you."

Kyle raised a brow. "Do you know how many times Cassie's apologized for introducing us? She even gave me permission to call her the worst sister ever during our last service trip with Jade. Why do you keep letting her come?"

"Even though you don't like her, Jade does work hard. It's only fair she gets to see some of her hard work on the other end." Deah took off her reading glasses. "This time she has gathered a group that includes fashion-design and construction-management majors. Both groups can be a great asset in the projects. They've already found some lightweight sewing machines and gathered fabric donations. Some of the older girls will enjoy learning to make their own clothes. I don't think any of them will be experts in a week, but sewing is a useful skill."

"So where does the artist fit in?"

"Oh, Araceli is the daughter of Dad's friend Rich. You met her once when you were about fourteen on a trip we took to New England."

Kyle thought for a moment. Surely not the round little girl with curly hair. "The family with the boy about my age and the two younger sisters?"

"Yes, that is the one. Araceli is about Cassie's age."

Marci bounced into the room. "EmilyAnne wants to go to Whataburger before the game. Can I have the car?"

"Who else are you going with?"

"Just us."

Kyle leaned forward. "Who are you meeting?"

Marci blushed and stuck out her tongue.

"Well, answer your brother's question. I seem to be off my parenting game tonight."

"A couple guys from school."

Deah frowned at the answer. "Do these guys have names?"

Kyle stood. "I sure am hungry. Whataburger sounds like an excellent idea."

"Mom!" Marci pushed at Kyle, trying to force him back onto the couch. "He can't go!"

Deah twirled her reading glasses. "Then I suggest you start by telling us some names."

"Grant and Liam. Y'all okay with that? I've known them for-ev-er." Marci crossed her arms.

"The car needs to be back in the garage a half hour after the game is over or I get a phone call explaining why not."

Marci bent and kissed her mother's cheek. "See ya!"

"Whataburger still sounds like dinner!" Kyle grinned at his mother.

"Don't you dare." Marci punctuated her statement by slamming the door.

"You shouldn't tease her like that. At least she has a date."

"Who says I don't?"

"You're hanging around here at five on a Saturday. That means you're bored out of your skull and your condo is way too quiet."

Kyle dropped back onto the couch. "Touché. Don't start. I need to find someone new. Half of the girls I know run at the mention of any type of service work. I need someone who enjoys it, because it's the work I love."

Deah laughed. "Maybe you should go on this trip. There are several women you haven't met, and we both know their reaction during the drive from the airport to the orphanage is an indicator of how well they will handle things."

"Not always. What about the family who moved down there after several visits and only lasted a week?"

"I still think you should come with us. Mother's intuition."

Kyle shook his head. "I registered for the conference in DC months ago. I really want to learn about some of the techniques for working with abused and trafficked children."

"Doesn't your conference end the day before we leave? You could change your flight and do both."

"Nope, I have plans to see the Capitol and meet up with some college friends."

"Female?"

"Nope." Kyle stood. "I think I'll head home. Maybe I'll stop at Whataburger on the way."

"Kyle, don't you dare. But if you do, let me know what you see."

Kyle kissed his mom's cheek. "Don't worry. It's more of a Tex-Mex night. When does Dad get home?"

"Sunday night."

"Come to dinner with me?"

Deah set her work aside. "You know I don't count as a date, right?"

"But you will always be my favorite."

An expression of mock horror filled Deah's face. "I hope not."

Kyle tossed his keys in the air. "I'll drive."

Sunday was one of Araceli's favorite days. When she was twelve, she heard a sermon about the Sabbath day and had never done homework on Sunday since. The day was reserved for calling family, being with friends, and reading books. To date, she held the record for the most books read in the house library. And she was the only one who felt put out when someone left their book on the table indicating Lover's Loft above the library was in use by a couple wishing private conversation. However, only Tessa was seriously dating anyone, and since Sean lived in Blue Pines, New York, *Tess of the D'Urbervilles* sat safely on the shelf next to *Far from the Madding Crowd*. Organization reigned supreme in the library. If only Araceli could organize the rest of her life the way she did her books.

She curled up on one of the couches with her laptop and sketch pad. Researching mural art and Haiti wasn't homework—just a way to pass time waiting for the weekly Sunday Williams family video call. Soon several open tabs lined the top of her browser. One of the problems was adding color, warmth, and interest to the orphanage without getting too busy. Many of the photos she found of Haiti included bright-but-busy painted trucks and busses and mural art on the many walls surrounding city buildings. A rough floor plan of the orphanage would help. It was hard to piece together the various photos to get an idea of the space.

Since she couldn't buy the paint in the United States and fly it down, she would have to work with the paint she could purchase there. Hopefully they had lead laws in Haiti. Since all the walls were cement, a household interior paint was her best option. An online search produced a couple of lumber and paint stores in Port-au-Prince. They did carry water-based paints. She opened another tab and studied the flat, stylized works of Préfète Duffaut.

Including the children in the painting process would be a challenge. What if she set up a paint-by-number-type thing? Several of the muralists she'd read about or watched on YouTube used chalk to sketch out the mural on the wall before beginning. The younger children would need help to paint in the lines. Then she could go back over the top and add in the details. If there were a couple of budding artists among the older children, they could help.

Araceli started some sketch ideas. Since she couldn't find enough similar words in Haitian Creole and French for the alphabet illustrations she ditched the alphabet idea in favor of zoo animals.

A chime sounded on her computer, and soon her screen was filled with video boxes of her parents' kitchen, her sister Amelia's dorm room, and her brother, Greg, and his wife and three-year-old, Max, at their home in New Hampshire. The usual greetings were exchanged, and updates were given. Araceli hoped she didn't look like her mind was wandering as Amelia detailed her experiments in chemistry. She saw something as she focused in on her mother's refrigerator. She then looked closely at the kitchen behind Greg. His fridge had it too. Araceli grew impatient for her turn. So what if Amelia's new formula burned three times longer? Apparently everyone but Araceli was enthralled. Finally, the spotlight moved to Araceli.

"Mom, what is hanging on your fridge?"

Terri got up and walked across the room. "A couple of wedding announcements, a picture you drew for Mother's Day when you were twelve, and Max's latest artwork from his visit last week. The usual, why?"

"Just a minute, Mom. Greg, what is on your fridge?"

Greg turned in his seat. "Alphabet magnets, Max's paper from preschool, and a drawing he claims is me but I think may really be an octopus."

"I think I know what the orphans in Haiti need—a refrigerator!"

Amelia sat forward. "Don't they have refrigerators in Haiti?"

"Yes, but that isn't what I mean. The children at the orphanage need a place to show off their work like we do on a refrigerator."

Greg's wife leaned toward the screen. "When I was little, my mom painted our playroom with all sorts of fun things. On one wall she made an art gallery where she painted picture frames with a white center the size of a piece of paper. We would hang all our masterpieces up." She turned to her husband. "I should do one for Max."

Hearing his name, Max ran over to the computer and commandeered the remainder of the family call.

Araceli wanted to ask how her sister-in-law had hung pictures in their playroom, but Greg signed off first, then Amelia.

"Dad, how would you make it so children could temporarily hang things on a wall?"

Rich Williams rubbed his goatee. "You could screw some bulldog clips to the wall. Or maybe glue some of the plastic sign holders to the wall so they could slip the drawings in and out."

"Thanks, Dad. Have a good week. Love you."

Araceli returned to looking at photos of the orphanage. How hard would it be to put one hundred or so screws in a cement wall?

four

ZOE HOOKED HER MESSENGER BAG over the chair next to Araceli. "What are you smiling at?"

"Mrs. Evans loves my idea of an art gallery for the children. I was worried because in the group chat, Jade, who has been on two other trips, said it wouldn't work. She kept going on and on about how they'd done that already. I think she may have even called me stupid in one of those 'bless your heart' Southern belle ways. So I thought there was no way my project would be approved. Not only was it approved, but it was picked for this trip."

"Now I need to find some way to hang the art. I looked at the plastic sign holders, but then all the artwork would have to be in the same direction, and who does everything landscape when you can choose portrait?"

Zoe pulled out her clipboard case, extracted some paper, and went into brainstorming mode. She fastened the paper under the clip. "What are your limitations?"

"The cement walls are the biggest, followed by size and trans-portability. I don't know what I am going to be able to buy down there. The Evanses are sending me two huge suitcases to fill with diapers, formula, and whatever I need for the murals."

1. Cement Walls

2. Weight

3. Size

4. Multiple sizes and orientations

5. Child safety

Zoe's neat handwriting resembled one of the architect type fonts. "What else?"

"That's about it. I didn't even think about child safety."

"What have you ruled out and why?"

"Bulldog clips, as they would have to be screwed into the wall and that's a lot of cement drilling. And I don't know how well they would stay. I have tried to come up with something magnetic, but everything is either too expensive or too bulky."

6. No screws

7. Magnetic?

Zoe tapped her pen against her chin. "What about those metal strips with the rollers in them? Dr. Christensen has some in his classroom where he puts up artwork for critiques."

"That is one idea. Do you know what they are called?"

Zoe shrugged. "Things they used to use to hold X-rays when they still used film?"

"Solid search terms." Araceli rolled her eyes and typed for a moment. "Nothing."

As Zoe pulled the paper off the clipboard, the clip on it snapped loudly. "Sorry, I don't think I helped much."

Araceli caught Zoe's wrist. "That's it! You're brilliant. Clipboards! They could be glued to the walls, and the children could even decorate them!"

"Glad I could help, even if it was the clipboard you all tease me about."

"Never again, Zoe!" Araceli searched office-supply websites.

"I'll give you a choice—take Marci dress shopping or lead the discussion with the spring-break group."

"It's a formal dance, isn't it?" Kyle tried to say the words without grimacing. At least Mom couldn't see his face through the phone.

"Don't make it sound like I'm sending you to the guillotine. It isn't Marci's fault that boy waited until the week before to ask her."

How many hundreds of shops would she have to go to? And the Galleria? No way was he going to hang around there watching his sister search for the perfect dress. "Just a video conference?"

"Like you've done before. Basic precautions, explanations, and answer questions."

"What time?"

"Five. I know some of the sorority girls have complained about how early the meeting is, but the part of Indiana Araceli Williams lives in is the eastern time zone. Thanks!"

"Hey, was that a siren I heard in the background? Are you and Marci already out shopping?" He should have realized it from the sound of engine noise when he first answered.

His sister's voice came over the phone. "You are the best, Kyle. Love you!"

The call disconnected.

He'd been played again.

He took his laptop over to the table he used for video conferences. The blank wall behind it served to keep people from being more interested in his choices of art than in his words.

He opened the conference program and was gratified to find the prerecorded presentation he usually used was queued and ready to go. The computer beeped as the participants logged on, their video feeds popping up in little boxes along the bottom of his screen. Other than Jade and Marci's friend EmilyAnne, he didn't recognize any of the group.

"It looks like everyone is here. I'm Kyle Evans. Deah asked that I conduct this video conference as she has an unexpected appointment. I'm assuming you have all read the information posted on the website, but there are a few things we need to cover. I'll take questions after the presentation. Please type them in the chat box." Once Kyle had switched the screen to display the prerecorded video, he studied the group's faces as it played. The woman listed as Chelsea turned green during a portion where they showed food vendors selling their wares only feet from a garbage pile covering nearly a quarter acre of land. A couple of the men looked squeamish during the segment on scabies. Only one of the volunteers appeared to be taking notes.

Kyle double-checked the screen. Araceli. Interesting. Mother told him he'd met her years ago, but the tiny face on the screen didn't match anything in his memory. But then, he only remembered befriending Greg. When the video presentation concluded, the questions were precisely what he expected. Unfortunately, Araceli didn't ask any, so her video screen remained the tiny thumbnail at the bottom of his screen. Shame. All he could discern of her was clear skin and a few dark curls escaping a ponytail or messy bun.

If he were conducting the service trip, he would turn it around and ask each of the volunteers a few questions himself. Then he could get a full-screen view of Araceli. As it was, Jade managed to commandeer the screen, not really asking a question at all.

"Jade, did you have a question? If not, I need to close the presentation."

"Oh no. Sorry, Kyle."

"If any of you have further questions, feel free to contact my mother. Good night."

Kyle clicked off the conference screen, opened the folder containing the volunteer applications, and found Araceli's.

As the screen went blank, Araceli released the first full breath she'd taken in the last half hour. At least she wouldn't have to see him again. Why did he have to grow up handsome? And his voice so confident, it was deeper than when they first met. His looks had sucked her in then too. But his unkindness had made her teen years so difficult. How was it possible to loathe and crush on the same person?

The doorbell rang, Araceli looked out the window to see a familiar brown delivery truck idling in the street in front of the house.

"Must be the last delivery of the night. Better than Santa." Candace opened the door and inspected the boxes. "Unless they aren't for me. Here, Araceli."

The first box contained two collapsible duffels for Haiti. The college group at her church had collected more than enough diapers and formula to fill both. Whatever wouldn't fit in the bags would be donated to the local women's crisis center.

The second box was from Grandma Williams. Araceli pulled out a package wrapped in paper decorated with candles and streamers.

"Did I goof? I thought your birthday was next month." Tessa pulled her phone out of her pocket.

"You didn't miss it. Grandma likes to send us early or late birthday gifts if she finds something she thinks we can use now rather than later."

Zoe perched on the corner of the couch. "So what did she get you?"

Araceli unwrapped the paper slowly, mostly to annoy her roommates, who watched her with the intensity of a Patriot's fan watching the Super Bowl. She held a fanny pack. "It has the RFID protection companies are putting in all the wallets now to keep people from electronically stealing passport and credit card information. The one she got me four years ago didn't have that feature. Only two and a half more weeks!"

"We know." Her roommates answered in unison.

MARCI JUMPED OUT OF THE chair she was sitting in and ran to Kyle's side as he rushed into the emergency room.

"Are you okay? Where is Mom?" Kyle studied her head to toe, looking for any signs of injury. The call his sister had made more than a half hour ago had been garbled. *Accident*, *police*, *ambulance*, and *Mom* had been the only discernable words. He had to ask her twice to repeat the name of the hospital before hopping in his car.

"I'm fine. I wasn't in the car yet. Mom was coming to pick me up. I heard the crash but didn't see it. She is back with the doctors. I haven't seen her since the ambulance brought her here." The wobble in her voice belied her insistence that she was okay.

Kyle drew his youngest sister into a hug.

Marci pushed back. "You can let go now."

Kyle took a step back.

Marci checked her phone. "I called Cassie. I figured I would wait to call Mark until we knew what was going on. Mom will have a fit if he hops a flight and misses class for her."

"He is at MIT, after all." Kyle smiled. "Is Cassie coming?"

"She said she would come downstairs as soon as another board member could fill in for the tour. Apparently she has some specialists in from Bombay."

The theme song to a sitcom played on the lobby TV. Kyle checked his watch.

Marci laid her head on his shoulder. "I've been here for almost an hour. When is Dad coming out?"

"Sorry I wasn't here earlier. The LBJ freeway was a parking lot." He rechecked his watch to see that only a minute had passed.

"Maybe we could find a quiet place to say a prayer. I have been praying in my mind, but it is so noisy."

Kyle took his sister by the hand and led her to the stairwell. "Is this good enough?"

When they returned, Cassie stood in the center of the ER waiting room with her hands on her hips. "Where have you two been?"

"We stepped out for a moment to pray." Marci's quiet answer took the impatience out of Cassie's face.

"They're taking Mom up for surgery. Dad asked me to show you where to go."

Kyle started to follow his sister. "When did you see Dad?"

"The assistant VP came in to relieve me about twenty minutes ago. I have been back with Mom and Dad ever since."

Marci slowed. "How did you get past us? We should have seen you."

Cassie swiped her hospital ID badge against a magnetic reader. "All-access pass. Hurry. If we go this way, we should be able to see Mom before they take her to the OR."

This sterile elevator was not the one Kyle had used the few times he'd visited the hospital. "Are we supposed to be here?"

"All-access pass, remember? If you are with me, no one will question it. I wouldn't take you any place y'all shouldn't be."

The elevator doors whooshed open, and Cassie led her siblings through a maze of halls to the back door of the surgery waiting room. They should bring Mom through here."

The bell on a different elevator pinged and their parents emerged, Mom on a gurney. Cassie gave Kyle the tiniest of superior nods. Dad looked haggard, but Mom wore a tired smile—the kind mothers used to reassure their families that a crisis was not insurmountable. From the raccoon-shaped bruises on her face, she'd been wearing sunglasses when the airbag deployed. Raising the hand with the IV in it, she gave them a small wave. Kyle barely heard her whispered "I love you."

Cassie ushered everyone into the waiting room.

Kyle fell in step behind his father. "What is the surgery for?"

"Let's all sit first, and I'll explain."

They found seats in the center of the room since the more desirable corners were already filled. "First, the good news. The doctors don't believe your mom has any internal injuries. The seat belt and airbags did their job. However, the impact crushed Mom's left clavicle and humerus. The clavicle fracture is compound, which is why they are not waiting for surgery."

"How long will she be in surgery?"

Dad patted Marci's knee. "I know they told me, but I can only think of the X-ray the doctor showed me—and your mom making some joke about officially having a screw loose."

They all gave a courtesy laugh.

"I know you kids have probably been praying since you got here, but let's have a family prayer before I call Mark."

Cassie jumped up. "Let me check if we can use one of the consultation rooms for a few minutes."

Dad turned to Kyle. "As you may guess, your mom was most worried about the trip to Haiti. With less than two weeks before departure, she doesn't want to cancel it."

Marci raised her head. "I don't know if I want to go without mom."

"Hey, squirt, I am not that bad of a guide, and you know you'll miss Marlissa if you don't go. Not to mention how much she will miss you."

Marci bit her lip. She'd sponsored Marlissa for the last four years. Most of the money she earned at her part-time job at the foundation went to pay for her special school for children with disabilities. Marlissa's vocabulary had grown by leaps and bounds. And last week's email hinted she had something exciting to show Marci. "As long as Mom is okay, I'll go. I really want to show EmilyAnne what we do down there. She's been learning some French and Haitian sayings so we can talk to the younger children."

Cassie returned. "We can use room three."

Kyle pondered the appropriateness of praying for a super-speedy recovery so he wouldn't have to lead the trip.

Packing for a week in a carry-on wasn't the easiest thing. Today's trip to the sporting-goods store supplied the clothing pretreatment to keep away the mosquitoes. The nurse at the county health department had recommended the spray when Araceli had visited to make sure she had all the necessary shots. Between Malaria and Zika virus, mosquitoes were among the most significant dangers. She also found a pack of repellant wipes. Any preventative that wasn't liquid and subject to TSA rules, especially if the item didn't take much space, was added to her list.

Her phone pinged, the incoming email marked urgent.

Spring-Break Service Group:

Friday night Mrs. Evans's car was struck by a truck. Doctors say she will recover. However, she will not be leading the service trip. I have decided to stay at home with her. Our son Kyle, who has been to Haiti over thirty times, will serve as the guide for the trip. If you have any questions, please message me.

F. Evans

PS. Please keep Deah in your prayers.

34

Kyle. Haiti. The ten-year-old self hiding in her brain screamed. She never wanted to be face-to-face with him again. She wasn't going to give him any control over her life again. He would not ruin this for her.

The chat app pinged.

> Tanner: Mrs. E, you are in our prayers.
>
> Jade: I can help Kyle if he needs it. Get well soon.
>
> Madison: Hugs and prayers.
>
> Chelsea: Oh, so sad :(Prayers
>
> Boyd: Mrs. E, get well soon.

Araceli reread the post before commenting with her well-wishes. Other than the video conference, she hadn't seen Kyle in nearly fourteen years, but the image of him and her brothers teasing her filled her mind. He probably wouldn't even remember. Men never did. She would pretend she didn't remember.

She shut her laptop and went in to watch TV. Anything to drown out the chanting in her head. She wasn't ten and had long grown out of the awkward preteen phase.

Nevertheless, "Celi-Belly shakes like jelly" managed to drown out the opening music to the rerun she brought up.

Too bad she didn't have a time machine. She would go back and spend all of fourth grade eating vegetables. Maybe he would have a crush on her this time and she could ignore him. She rolled her eyes at herself. She had as much chance of that as the canned laughter coming from the TV sounding real. After all, she'd dumped a full bowl of lime Jell-O over his head in retaliation. *Kyle, Kyle, looks like bile.* But he hadn't reacted then any more than he had on last week's conference call. No wonder Jade was chasing after him. He'd changed in appearance, cute morphing into handsome. Maybe he'd changed inside, too.

Kyle checked his watch as the applause faded and the keynote speaker left the stage. Just enough time to make it to the airport. He'd hoped to have a few minutes to catch up with a colleague he hadn't realized was here until the closing session, but missing the plane wasn't an option. The red-eye would get him back to DFW too late to drive to his condo to change clothes and swap suitcases for the morning flight to Haiti.

Kyle waved at his friend and was headed for his rental car when his phone rang. His mother's smiling face appeared on the screen.

"Hey, Mom. How are you feeling?"

"Only two pain killers so far today. I wanted you to know Cassie isn't going. She managed to find a flu strain not covered by this year's vaccine."

"Marci?"

"We all got tested. No one else has it. Are you going to spend the night here?"

"No, I was going back to my condo. Do you need me to get Marci and EmilyAnne?"

"I'll have the car service drop them off at the terminal. I wanted to see you before you left."

"My flight gets into DFW at ten. Will you be up if I drop by then?"

"As long as I can find a movie to watch." Her voice sounded tired.

"See you in a few hours. Love ya, Mom."

Kyle started his car and pulled out of the lot, mentally reassigning the things Cassie was going to do in Haiti. Anything medical related would have to wait for another trip. Marci was going to update photos of all the children, and any of the volunteers could help with growth photos as well as inventories.

By the time he got to the airport, the left side of his head was starting to throb.

He prayed the person in seat 3B wasn't a talker.

six

THE LAST TORNADO HAD CAUSED less damage than this. Araceli looked around at the disaster that was her room. Debris lay everywhere. Every drawer open and empty. Every box pulled out from under the bed. Her clothing was strewn across every surface, and her furniture had been moved, exposing a multitude of three-year-old dust bunnies. Her beloved teddy-bear collection had been uprooted from its place and was now lying in a heap near the closet door. The disaster had taken most of the night to create, and now Araceli sat on her bed, forcing back the tears. She needed to leave for the Fort Wayne airport in a half hour. She'd packed everything—her airline ticket, her money, her repellent.

Everything but her passport.

"Araceli, are you ready?" Tessa paused in the doorway.

"I can't find my passport. I know I put it somewhere safe, but I can't remember where safe was. I can't think of anyplace else to look. I keep trying to be more organized, but—" She waved her arm at the room.

Tessa stepped over a pile of clothing by the door. "I've seen worse. Sean's grandfather's house is a hoarder's paradise. When did you last see your passport?"

"The day I ordered my plane tickets."

"So, you were here at your desk, and where was your passport then?"

"In my second drawer. That was the first place I looked." Araceli leaned over and flipped through a pile of stuff before returning it to the empty drawer.

Tessa poked around the room. A few things still hid in the shadows of the walk-in closet. She turned on the light, revealing a formal dress, two coats, a box marked "Shoes," and a large suitcase. She checked the shoebox first. "I am not asking why you have a box of mismatched gloves." Tessa pulled out the suitcase. "Any chance it could be in here?"

"My old suitcase?" Araceli joined Tessa in the closet and unzipped the bag, pulling out her old fanny pack. "Tessa, you are brilliant!" She hugged the passport to her chest.

Tessa pointed to the clock. "Made it with ten minutes to spare!"

Araceli picked up a pile of clothes and moved it to her bed. "Candace is going to take away my deposit when she sees this."

"Shut the door and hope you beat her back. She left with Zoe for the week to that living-history-retreat thing Zoe's mom set up. Since Candace is not into family history and annoyed over the DAR thing, she might not notice your room for a day or two."

"Dar?"

"Daughters of the American Revolution. She thinks this trip will be a disaster, like last summer's Society of Indiana Pioneers pilgrimage."

"The one with the Ohio River cruise, right? She came back with that saying about genealogists disturbing the dead and annoying the living."

"Yup, so she might not notice the room if she gets on one of her rants. I see red-white-and-blue wigs in the future."

Araceli kicked a pile of clothes out of the way and shut her door. "Port-au-Prince, here I come."

"Come on. If I miss my 6:00 a.m. plane to JFK and even a half day with Sean, you might pray Candace finds your room."

The best thing about the predawn flight was that DFW was not busy yet. The worst was that Jade and two other girls had yet to show up. Kyle looked at the eight bags waiting to be checked. Due to airline limitations, it was essential each passenger be responsible for two of the large duffels. Diapers, formula, and various other supplies requested by the orphanage had been packed, along with three sewing machines, several bolts of fabric, thread, an electric drill, and donated paint brushes. The other members of the group had checked their two assigned bags and gone through TSA with Marci fifteen minutes ago.

Next to him, the automatic doors opened with a whoosh. Kyle breathed a short-lived sigh of relief to see the missing girls. He automatically looked at his watch. Twenty minutes late. Thankfully his mother always built in enough time to compensate.

"Don't look at me that way. You know Deah builds in extra time." Jade brought three bags to a halt in front of him.

"Jade, what is that bag? You know you are only allowed two carry-on items." Kyle eyed a third carry-on.

"Oh, this? Just a few last-minute things I found to take down. You know how much fun those girls had last year with the crafts I brought."

Fun? Not how he remembered it. "You can't take three carry-ons."

"I'm not. I was going to stuff this in the checked bags."

"Each of these bags has been weighed to the ounce. You can't put anything in them."

Jade pushed out her lower lip. "You would deny the children?"

Instead of appearing sexy, her pout reminded him of his grand-ma's saying: "If you don't put your lip back where it belongs, a bird will come poop on it." Kyle kept the thought to himself. "This is your third trip with us. You know the rules. I am giving you two choices. March up to the counter and check these two bags the way they have been packed and figure out how to consolidate your three carry-ons into two before our flight leaves, or call an Uber and go home. You can drop these two bags off at my parents' home and explain to Mom why you felt you were above the rules. Warning—she is still in quite a bit of pain and refuses to take anything stronger than acetaminophen."

Jade looked at each of her friends. "I am sure we can find enough room in everyone's carry-ons for this stuff. TSA won't stop me for three bags, will they?"

"I don't think they count bags." Kyle gave the overloaded luggage cart a shove. "Ladies, after you."

He managed to bite his tongue until the cabin doors shut and the passenger-safety monologue had commenced. He sat next to Marci and EmilyAnne, the only minors on the trip. "Please, when you go to college, don't turn into her."

Marci looked over her shoulder at the row behind them. "I can't believe she talked those guys into putting her stuff in their bags. But then, they probably don't pack the way you do. I don't think you could even stick a piece of gum in your bag. Please tell me you at least brought two changes of clothes with all the other things you packed for the orphans."

"I'll have you know I brought a full week's worth of clothing. Why don't you get some sleep? You were up as long as I was last night." Kyle had reached his parents' house only to find Marci three hours into the five-hour version of *Pride and Prejudice* with Mom.

His sister yawned. "With the layover in Atlanta, we don't land until 2:00 p.m. in Haiti. Are we even going to get out to the orphanage and back before dark?"

"By the time we get out of the airport, we'll have four hours of daylight. Just enough time to go drop off all the donations, hand out hugs, and check the supplies we ordered."

"We could wait until tomorrow."

Kyle leaned into the headrest for takeoff. "The children are expecting us. Now sleep." He closed his eyes.

The Atlanta airport was bustling with passengers hurrying to catch their flights. How many flights landed late, like hers? Araceli looked at the flight board and map. Twenty minutes until takeoff. What if she missed her flight?

The seconds ticked by as she waited for the train to Terminal E and her gate. Recorded announcements played overhead, and she looked at her phone. Eleven minutes. A bell sounded, and passengers crowded off the train and she boarded, her anxiety spiking as she looked at her watch again. How far would she need to run to E6?

The doors flew open, a family exiting before her. Araceli skirted them and ran for the escalator. As she neared the top, she heard the announcement "Will passenger Williams please check in at gate E6?" It took only a second for her to orient herself before she took off at a sprint. Gasping for air, she zigged around an older couple and zagged around a stroller. Why had she not been more diligent about her exercise? A man stood in front of E6, waving and motioning for her to hurry, as if he expected her to reach Supergirl speeds.

As she passed E8, her right lung threatened to collapse, every breath burning, but she kept running. Closer now, she recognized Kyle Evans, his arms beckoning.

"Araceli?"

Her lungs and muscles were screaming. It was entirely possible she'd broken her own four-hundred-meter record. Nodding was the best she could do. Great. She'd wanted to make a good impression. Prove to him she wasn't an awkward ten-year-old anymore. Instead, she was going to collapse at his feet.

He didn't touch her as he escorted her to the door. She probably smelled like she felt. Feeling the perspiration run down her back, she wished she could change her shirt.

"Boarding pass? Passport?" asked the uniformed attendant.

Kyle handed his passport and ticket over. Araceli dug in her fanny pack and thrust hers into the employee's outstretched hand.

"Our flight is very full. We'll need to gate check your carry-on. Is there anything you need from it?"

Still unable to answer, Araceli shook her head. The employee affixed a tag to the handle, and they entered the Jetway, the door shutting behind them.

Kyle took the rolling bag from her. "Let me." He hurried ahead of her to where a man in uniform coveralls and orange ear protectors awaited their bags.

"What seat?"

"Thirty-two C." The words came out in a breathless heap.

"I'm 31D." Kyle gestured for her to board first.

Araceli nodded. She counted down the rows, looking for her seat, but none of the aisle seats were empty. A blonde about her age sat in hers, chatting to the man across the aisle. Araceli double-checked her ticket. "Excuse me. I believe this is my seat."

The woman glanced up. Jade. She looked more like a model in person than she did on the conference calls. "You could sit there." She gestured to the middle seat, not making any effort to stand or let Araceli in.

"Jade, move over." A disapproving voice sounded over Araceli's shoulder.

Jade was not going to steal her seat. Araceli needed to get up as soon as the seat-belt sign went off to be the first in line for the lavatory—a luxury denied her by her delayed flight.

An attendant came from the back of the plane. "Is there something wrong here?" she asked in heavily accented English.

In answer, Araceli held up her boarding pass.

The attendant turned to Jade. "May I see your boarding pass?" The woman studied it for a moment. "You are supposed to be in 34B." The attendant looked back two rows.

A man no older than twenty-one raised his hand. "I had 32B and traded her."

The attendant looked down at the blonde. "Please move to the center seat so this woman can sit down and we can depart. We've already held the plane longer than we should have."

For a moment, Araceli thought Jade wouldn't comply and would have to be dragged off the plane. Visions of viral videos flashed through her head. And somehow they would make it seem like Araceli's fault.

But Jade unbuckled her seat belt and moved over.

"Move your bag, too, miss." Directed the attendant as she pointed to a bag in front of the aisle seat.

"But under my seat is already full."

"Then hand me one of your bags, and I will gate check it."

As Jade pulled the bag in front of 32C out and stuffed it under 32B, she flashed Araceli a look that made her think of the type of retaliation mean girls planned in high school. Conscious of dozens of eyes on her, Araceli took her seat, not even pulling her paperback out of her backpack before stowing it. The in-flight magazine would have to do until the fasten-seat-belt light changed.

She looked up to see Kyle looking over his shoulder and mouthing "Sorry."

Araceli nodded and managed a smile, which he returned before turning forward in his seat. It wasn't like Jade's behavior was his fault. Although, if Jade's chat-room claims were true, they were an item. Maybe she could pretend he was apologizing for teasing her all those years ago. Because her old crush was pounding on her heart to be let back in.

Next to her, Jade stirred. "Save yourself the effort. Kyle Evans doesn't go for the artistic type."

This was going to be a very long flight. Araceli imagined what she would like to say as the plane backed out of the gate. *Hey, Catty, I am not too sure why you think you can steal my seat, demean my project-idea, and control whether or not I can speak with Kyle. But I am going to Haiti to see if I can make a difference in this world—not to flirt, and not to please you. So if you don't mind, let's decide now to ignore each other as much as possible. You help the children your way, and I will do it mine.* Instead, she plastered on a smile that would have made Candace proud. "Thanks for the advice. But as with my mural idea, I think I can decide for myself."

"If you don't want my help, fine. I didn't want you getting hurt. I am still surprised Deah approved your idea to be one of the projects. My project has been put on hold for the family groups. I bet you haven't ever tried to paint with children. It gets so messy. As far as your seat, you were late, and I saw you checking out Kyle, so I wanted you to know he was taken. Saving you pain later."

Interested in Kyle? Oh, please. Taking her own advice and ignoring Jade, Araceli opened the magazine.

Jade turned to the woman in the window seat and conversed in low tones. As the plane gathered speed and lifted off the runway, Araceli's heart beat a little faster. Next stop—Port-au-Prince!

Either getaways to the Alaskan frontier were Araceli's thing or she was excellent at ignoring annoying people. Kyle studied Araceli's reflection in his phone screen for a few more seconds. She barely resembled the old vacation photo he found. Her hair was longer and darker but still curly. At least she hadn't straightened it. Haiti's humidity would curl the spirals tighter. He wondered how springy they were. When he'd seen Araceli sprinting for the gate, he couldn't reconcile her with the chubby ten-year-old he'd met almost a decade and a half ago. From the way she ran, he assumed track was her sport of choice, and for an artist, she was sensibly dressed.

He sneaked another peek only to see her seat empty. The fasten-seat-belt sign was off. A glance over his shoulder confirmed she was joining the line for the lavatory. Kyle unbuckled his seat belt and hurried down the aisle.

"Sorry about the seat thing."

Araceli half turned and gave him a shrug. "I am glad she moved. I was afraid it would become another viral airline incident."

He couldn't come up with a name for the shade of her light-brown eyes. They reminded him of the last few drops of root beer hiding between the ice of an empty cup. "Your sprint to the plane was impressive. I didn't think you would make our flight when your flight was delayed."

"What would have happened then?"

"I would have waited for you. My sister Marci would have gotten everyone to the orphanage and then the guesthouse. She's been on enough trips to navigate, and she speaks both French and Haitian Creole."

"Why didn't Marci wait for me?"

"This is going to sound sexist, but after you experience Haiti for a few hours, maybe you will understand. Letting two young single white females navigate from the airport to the guesthouse after dark would not be very responsible."

She crossed her arms. "You're right. It sounds sexist."

"Aren't there parts of Boston your father would feel the same way about?"

Araceli bobbed her head in answer and changed places with the passenger exiting the lavatory area.

Fifteen minutes later, the snack cart came by, and Kyle ordered a root beer. Marci looked at his glass. "I thought you preferred ginger ale."

"I did."

seven

For the third time, Kyle passed word back for everyone to wait at the end of the Jetway when they got inside the airport. Araceli wondered how used to going to Haiti Kyle really was, or did he think the group couldn't process taking orders? She looked out the corner of her eye at Jade and the woman who'd finally introduced herself as Chelsea. They seemed to be in another world. Maybe he should repeat his orders a fourth time.

That wasn't fair to Chelsea. She did seem adept at listening. Araceli wished she had been able to meet the group in person before the flight. The group was easy enough to pick out. Most of the passengers were likely Haitian from the smattering of French she heard mixed in with what she assumed was Haitian Creole. To be honest, the dozen Caucasian twenty-somethings in their group stood out like marshmallows in a giant cup of hot chocolate. Blending in wasn't much of an option. There was a smaller group of Caucasians consisting of middle-aged men and women all wearing matching T-shirts further up the cabin. Araceli assumed they were also on some type of service mission.

As the plane started its final descent, Araceli caught snatches of lush green hillsides outside the window next to Chelsea. Little buildings lay clustered close together. The ocean's cool blue water looked inviting. Cutting off Araceli's view, Chelsea and Jade crowded the window, with Jade pointing out various landmarks.

Araceli sat back in her seat. She would see Haiti soon enough.

Kyle looked over his shoulder at her. "I'll make sure you get a window seat on the way out if you want. It is more fun to see when you know what the view looks like from the ground."

"Thanks."

As the thump-thump of the landing gear shook the plane, adrenaline pumped through Araceli's veins and she had to resist the urge to squeal with delight. They were here. As they taxied to the terminal, Araceli caught a glimpse of the airport. Perhaps that was just the international wing. There was no way an international airport could be smaller than the one she'd flown out of in Fort Wayne.

Chelsea turned to Jade. "The airport is so tiny!"

"Welcome to PAP. No big shiny airport here when this will do. Wait until you see the inside. They could film an old '70s movie there."

"I guess I expected the airport to be modern."

Jade laughed at her friend's comment.

So the airport was smaller than Fort Wayne's—not that she expected something the size of Boston's Logan airport.

When they'd all gathered at the end of the Jetway, Kyle counted heads before he spoke. "Bathrooms are over there. I suggest you use them as it will be two or three hours before you see another one. Remember, do not flush the toilet paper or anything else. Everyone needs to get their passport and five dollars out to pay the entry tax before we go through customs at the desk at the end of the hall." He gestured to the other side of the room. "If anyone tries to take your bag once we are out of the customs area, say, 'Non, merci!' as firmly as you can as many hundred times as you need to. Do not let anyone take your luggage. Before we leave the airport, have a firm grip on all your bags."

Each stall in the bathroom contained a large garbage can full of used toilet paper. No wonder sanitation was such an issue here. Araceli had read about the poor sanitation infrastructure, but experiencing it was another thing. She followed the other group members through paying the entry tax and customs.

One of the guys, Boyd, if he matched his photo, held up the small paper he'd received at the tourist tax desk. "What am I supposed to do with this?"

Jade answered before anyone else could. "Keep the paper with your passport. We have never needed it on other trips, but just in case."

"What she said." Kyle counted the bags and containers, then motioned to two of the guys. "Go get a couple of carts, and remember, 'Non, merci' if someone tries to help." He looked down at his phone. "Our drivers are here."

The guys returned and loaded most of the checked baggage onto the carts.

Kyle lined them up like an army marching into battle. "Ryan, go last with Marci. She speaks enough Creole to address any issues we have getting out of the airport. Araceli, if you can take Boyd's extra bag, and Chelsea if you take Tanner's, I think we have everything. Let's go."

Araceli tried not to roll her eyes at Kyle's overprotective attitude. She assumed everyone had flown before and probably internationally. Dragging her wheeled carry-on and pushing Boyd's in front of her, she fell in line behind him and the heavy cart he was pushing. Not two feet out the door to the parking lot, a skinny man in a dirty T-shirt tried to take Boyd's bag from her.

"Non, merci."

The man walked beside her and tried again. Araceli would have stepped out of the way, but the sidewalk was lined with men trying to do the same thing, so she held on to the bags and raised her voice. "Non, merci!"

Traversing the twenty yards to the parking lot, Araceli joined the others in shouting "Non, merci!" and shaking her head at the dozen or so men reaching for their luggage. No one had told her entering Haiti required running a gauntlet. She reevaluated Kyle's overprotectiveness.

In a parking lot only slightly larger than that of a typical chain-restaurant, Kyle directed them to two large vans and an SUV. "Don't let your bags go until you hand them to the drivers. Boyd, Tanner, take the carts to the blue van."

The overly helpful men followed them nearly to the vans, still trying to take their luggage, until the drivers shouted at the men in Creole, and the men left in the direction of the terminal. Kyle hugged one of the drivers and asked him about his wife and new baby, then shook hands with the other two. A fourth driver appeared and also received a hug. Marci joined her brother in both giving hugs and exchanging greetings.

Loading of the vans became a game of 3-D Tetris. Not once did Kyle or the drivers pull out a bag or rearrange them. "The blue van is going directly to the orphanage. Marci, you and EmilyAnne go with that one, please. Tanner and Boyd, you can go with them. Marci, you remember where the bags go so the kids don't get into them first?"

Marci gave a mock salute. "What about the eggs?"

"I put them in the bin with the yellow lid. They will go to the guesthouse."

Eggs? They'd transported eggs on the plane? Araceli was sure one of the books she'd read talked about the plethora of roosters on the island. Why would they need eggs?

"The black van is going to the guesthouse first. Jade, will you be in charge of that van? Put things where Mrs. Delino tells you and don't worry about rooms. I'd like to get everyone to the orphanage this afternoon, so drop off the stuff as fast as you can."

Jade pulled Chelsea and the two other guys in the group, Brandon and Ryan, into the van.

Kyle turned to the remaining women. "Madison, Kate, and Araceli, you are with me in the SUV. We are going to pick up the bottled water."

Kyle sat in the front with the driver, whom he introduced as Aselòm. Araceli took the seat between the other two women. The vans inched out of the parking lot and past the last stop sign they would see for the rest of the day. They passed brick wall after brick wall, some plastered with graffiti and ads or colorful murals, though most were gray cinder block and topped with concertina wire. Every once in a while, they could see inside a gate to a business or church.

Tap taps, the brightly painted busses and converted pickup trucks that served as the city's transportation, passed them going either direction on what Araceli assumed was meant to be a two-lane road but was actually five disorganized lanes. As she watched motorcycles zip between the cars, Madison pointed to one of the tap taps. Flat, hand-shaped metal spikes stuck out at right angles near tire level, threatening to scratch a car or pop the tires of any impatient driver who dared drive too close. Every inch of the tap taps was painted in bright colors in various themes, one boasting movie stars, including John Wayne and Humphrey Bogart. Others were of a religious nature. Almost all of them, including the one covered with '80s rock stars, featured a variation of *"Mèsi Jezi"* written somewhere on them.

"What does Mèsi Jezi mean?" Kate asked.

Kyle turned in the front seat. "'Thank you, Jesus.' You will also see the phrase in French as well as in English on them. I have heard it's because the drivers are thankful they didn't crash today. And now y'all know what happens to all those trucks and school buses that die in the States."

"Resurrected in Haiti?" Kate pointed at a *Gone With the Wind*–themed tap tap.

Beep! Beep!

Honk!

Araceli followed the progression of one of the motorcycles. "All of the different honks. It is like a different language."

Aselòm laughed. "Miss Marci says she make a honk dictionary so she can translate all of them."

They came to an intersection of five roads, all the vehicles trying to cross at the same time. Horns blared. A motorcycle wove through traffic. Araceli expected a crash at any second as a pickup-sized tap tap sped past a black sedan with diplomatic flags. There was no clear flow of traffic in any direction, no stop signs, no one giving directions. She had been in traffic jams in Boston, but they had an order and symmetry to them. Their driver honked and moved forward, cutting off a bus with a giant face of Tom Selleck painted on the side.

"Where are the stop signs?" Araceli wondered out loud.

The driver answered. "No stop signs here."

Madison's white knuckles contrasted with the arm of the seat she was gripping. "Are there traffic laws?"

Kyle turned in his seat. "You might want to refer to them as 'guidelines.' I think in the fifteen years I have been coming here, I have only seen a policeman pull a car over twice. The good thing about the traffic moving so slowly is most car accidents are not deadly, though the ones involving the motorcycles are often tragic. It can take a half hour or longer for emergency personnel to arrive. That is why we caution all our teams to never take the motorcycle taxis."

The driver turned between two tall cinder-block walls into a parking lot.

Holding back a smile at the women's reactions, Kyle followed them past the guard and into the grocery store. He never got tired of watching the surprise on volunteer faces when they saw American brands and foods and prices listed in dollars. The women walked around the produce, talking in hushed tones. Already he was guessing how well the women would adapt to the country. Kate's face showed relief at seeing the familiar brands. She might survive the trip, but she would not be back. Between her white knuckles during the ride and her careful study of the store, Madison could go either way. Then there was the one who took everything in. Araceli would come back if she could.

He watched her study the mangoes.

Kyle picked one up. "We will have them almost every morning at breakfast, so you don't need to buy any." He picked up a banana-like fruit. "These are plantains. They fry them into delicious chips—one of the few things I purchase from the street vendors."

Madison and Kate joined them.

Kyle directed them to the far side of the cash registers. "Let's buy the water. We will bring everyone back to the store the day before we fly out. The Haitian vanilla is one thing I suggest taking home as a gift for your favorite cook." Kyle led them over to the drink aisle.

Madison picked up a cola bottle. "Hey, this is made with real sugar. I haven't seen that since the plant out in Dublin closed." She grabbed two other bottles. "My caffeine and sugar fix for the next three days."

Kyle hefted four cases of water into the cart and grabbed a Limonade. "This is one of my favorites—it's like lemonade but better."

All three women grabbed a bottle.

"Remember to pay in the lowest denomination American dollars possible. They will give you change in Haitian gourde." Kyle pulled out his phone and turned on the calculator app. "The dollar is worth roughly sixty-five gourdes."

"This is why you told us to bring so many dollar bills, right?" Madison handed the cashier four dollars.

"Yes. Almost everyone accepts USD. The last day, we will take you to a street market and you can spend your accumulated gourde there if you don't get to the store. If we go to the hardware store, you will see most prices listed in dollars."

The group exited the building past a glowering guard and climbed into their car.

Kate settled into her seat and nodded to the door they'd come through. "He looked ominous."

Araceli climbed into the back seat. "I read they had huge problems with theft in Haiti, but it's odd to see an armed guard at the grocery store."

"Most Haitians make less than three dollars a day. The minimum wage income is about $800 a year. So as you can imagine, the cola Madison is drinking right now is out of most people's budgets—especially if they have children, as school costs $500 or more per year, per student."

Madison took a sip of her cola. "Wow, so someone would need to work a half day to buy this drink. That really puts it in perspective. To think I complained about minimum wage when I was in high school."

"In January I took a custodial job to help pay for this trip. Working part-time for a month, I made about $800."

"You mean you cleaned toilets to come here?" Madison made a face.

"Rather ironic, isn't it. Cleaning toilets to come to a country where the plumbing is suspect." Araceli laughed, a rich sound that made Kyle swivel in the seat so he could see if her smile dimpled.

It did.

Kyle turned forward again and wondered why he'd thought she would have dimples when she laughed. A memory of playing a version of Uno that shot cards out of a dispenser came flooding back. No, way! Kyle tried not to turn and look at her again. The girl from his memory had followed him and her brother Greg around most of the vacation, her attraction to him as obvious as it was uncomfortable, especially with Greg's comments and kissing noises. She was cute enough for a girl, but he'd acted like the stupid teenage boy he was and made her cry. He must have suppressed the memory.

Someone asked about the bridge they were crossing. Kyle didn't answer, so the driver told how once, a mighty river had rushed under the bridge but disappeared after the 2010 earthquake. The two-lane bridge was one of the few ways to cross the nearly empty gorge.

The song Kyle had made up to get the girl to leave him alone popped into his head. Remorse twisted his gut. He recapped his drink and thought of Marci and how he'd wanted to punch the guy who'd made fun of her braces in seventh grade because it made her cry. An apology was long overdue. As a therapist, he knew how something like what he'd said and done could emotionally stunt someone for life. At least she seemed normal. But the hurt could be hidden.

Had the girl he'd dubbed Celi-Belly forgiven him?

eight

THE PHOTOS ARACELI HAD SEEN online didn't do the island nation justice. The bright colors that now permeated the car windows were stunning. Women in dresses balanced baskets and various bundles on their heads. Men hefted bags of water and foodstuffs she didn't recognize into the slow-moving cars. Other than the bridge they crossed over, the cars, tap taps, and motorcycles didn't stay within the lanes as they made their way around parked busses and vendors. Araceli's imagination failed to see what could be hiding behind the cinderblock walls and solid metal gates, though some proclaimed in both French and English that a school or a hospital lay beyond.

Aselòm turned onto a narrow, rutted dirt track resembling more of a gorge than a street. Half-built cinder-block houses dotted the sides. Barefoot children toted jugs of water in wagons or balanced them on their heads. The SUV bounced and dipped. The women held on to the doors and to each other, hoping the vehicle would not tip on its side as it traversed the sharply angled road. Surely there wouldn't be an orphanage up here.

A delivery truck exited a gate a hundred yards ahead and came barreling toward them. Araceli wondered how it had gotten up the road, a generous term, in the first place. Their driver pulled the SUV as high up on the banked side of the road as he could to let the truck pass. Her heart racing at the close call, Araceli studied the building beyond the still-open gate. It was some type of warehouse. How could trucks traverse such a road daily?

They turned a corner and beyond possibility found a dirt road in poorer condition than the one they'd been on. Aselòm angled to cross a drainage pipe that lay half exposed. A cringe-inducing scrape of metal on cement filled the vehicle.

"Next time, you will need to get out for us to cross here. The last rain did too much damage."

Kyle spoke for the first time in a while. "Can we fill in the dip?"

Aselòm shrugged. "The rain will just wash it out again."

The car turned another corner, over a ten or twelve foot cinder-block wall Araceli could see what she assumed was the third floor of the orphanage. The driver honked at the gate.

Someone on the other side rolled it back, and they drove into a large yard surrounded on all four sides by one of the ever-present wire-topped cinder-block walls.

The driver honked at a second gate. When it opened, the bottom of the SUV scraped against the metal grate as it dipped into the next yard.

"That one we will fix," said Kyle as he rolled down the window and waved back the children who swarmed the vehicle.

"Mr. Kyle! Mr. Kyle!" the children yelled and waved.

Kyle turned in his seat. Make sure you lock your doors when you get out and keep your phones hidden. They love to play with them."

As soon as the driver stopped the SUV, Kyle hopped out and, like a piece of candy attracting a swarm of ants, was surrounded by dozens of children all speaking at once.

Araceli climbed out of the car, followed by Madison, who barely got the door shut before children surrounded them.

Marci came out of the huge three-story concrete building balancing a toddler on each hip. "Come on, I'll give y'all the quick tour." She looked in the direction of her brother. "Kyle will be busy until we leave. He will want to say hello to every single child, and most of them will need to tell him a story. The older ones will want to practice their English on you."

As they entered the maze of rooms, Araceli doubted she would be able to locate the kitchen or office areas again without help. The nursery would be easy to find, as with nineteen babies some-one was bound to cry. Marci encouraged each of the girls to pick up one of the little ones.

"At this age they need love. There are not enough workers to hold them as much as a mother would. So when I am doing something that isn't dangerous, I try to give a couple of cuddles." She paused where a girl sat on what resembled a wide skateboard. "Marlissa, meet my new friends—Araceli, Kate, and Madison." The little girl waved. "Marlissa just turned ten and has a surprise for me, but she won't tell me yet."

Marlissa covered her mouth with her hands and shook her head. Marci waved to her and continued the tour.

They skipped the children's dormitories as they were off-limits to visitors. Any repairs that needed to be done in the area would be completed once the children were at school.

They passed several girls washing laundry in large tubs or hanging it out to dry. Marci spoke to many of them by name as they crossed the courtyard to the kitchen area. Here, three women and several older girls bustled about, preparing dinner for the nearly one hundred residents not fed in the nursery.

One of the side rooms contained three sizeable front-loading washers and dryers.

"Why don't they use these to do all the laundry?" asked Araceli.

"The electrical in this room isn't equipped to handle the current needed. I think there is something they need to do to rewire it for the washers and dryers. The sad thing is, they were donated nearly a year ago."

Madison ran her hand over the top of one of the dryers and looked at her palm. No dust. "I think Boyd has done quite a bit of electrical work. We should ask him to check out this room."

"That would be nice. You can imagine how much laundry we generate with the sheets and towels."

Marci led Madison, Kate, and Araceli through another maze of halls and out the front door, where the other volunteers had gathered in the front yard and were mingling with the children. From the back of the building, a cowbell rang several times. Some of the children snuck in one more hug with Kyle or Marci before running to dinner, but the majority took off at the sound of the bell.

Kyle pointed to the two vans. "We can all pile in. Dinner is waiting for us at the guesthouse."

Araceli followed Marci into one of the vans only to end up in the center back seat. Jade took the window seat in front of her in the middle row.

Marci rolled her eyes as Jade started a running commentary that ended when the driver honked in front of the gate of the guesthouse nearly an hour later.

Dinner was a mix of Haitian and American foods. Mrs. Delino had planned the perfect first night's meal. The guesthouse was one of the hidden treasures of Port-au-Prince. Mrs. Delino had come to Haiti years ago to work at one of the hospitals. In time, she'd fallen in love with Martin and they were married. The biracial couple was on oddity in Haiti. It was perhaps because of this that they ran the best guesthouse in the country.

Judging by the lack of conversation, either everyone appreciated the food or was tired beyond words. Kyle decided to make a few announcements. "If you did not treat your sleeping clothes with mosquito repellent, I advise you to spray a bit on them before sleeping. Even the mosquito netting lets a few through.

The essential oils some of you brought, like lavender, will also repel mosquitoes. Besides, lavender is supposed to help you sleep and is preferable to the smell of DEET. There is a men's and a women's dormitory-style room. As we have two minors on this trip, I am going to be strict in that respect. If you want to talk and mingle, use the lower-level family room or terrace."

Marci groaned but didn't comment.

"Tomorrow, one van will be going to the lumber store to pick up the items we need. The other will go straight to the orphanage. Both will be leaving at 8:00 a.m. sharp. EmilyAnne and Marci, will you go in the van with Boyd, Ryan, and Brandon to get the wood and supplies? A driver will meet you there with a truck to help haul what you need. Also, you can rent the tools they need from the other place, but send the driver to be the interpreter. I don't want you to go in if it can be avoided, as he will charge you double since you are American. Any questions?"

Jade raised her hand. "I thought I was getting one of the suites this time. Deah said there would be one available."

Kyle shook his head. "No, we only rented the dorm rooms. Mrs. Delino called last week. A couple who is trying to adopt needed to come down last minute. Mom let the suite go. Anyone else?"

Several people shook their heads. Marci raised her hand. "Since Cassie isn't here, I thought I would remind everyone to wear their flip-flops in the shower. Even though they clean this guesthouse very well, some of the parasites still may be around."

"All of you should be thankful Marci gave a condensed form of Cassie's lecture. See y'all at breakfast."

Kyle stayed near the table, hoping to catch a word with Araceli. Unfortunately, Jade took it as an opportunity to flirt with him, and Araceli went up the stairs with the girls she'd spent most of the day with. Was she avoiding him?

nine

SATURDAY MORNING AT THE ORPHANAGE was like Saturday morning with Max times one hundred. Children ran around chatting in Haitian, French, and English. Several of the fourteen- to sixteen-year-olds spoke English well enough that Marci tasked them with being junior interpreters.

Araceli used her rusty French to answer the multitude of questions. Fortunately, André, the teen Marci asked to interpret for Araceli, delighted in speaking English and told her and Madison about absolutely everything as he led the small entourage to a second-floor storeroom where the donated supplies for painting were kept. The little room was crammed full of boxes and battered suitcases.

One shelf held a stack of children's winter clothing. Araceli wondered if they needed the flannel and fleece wear. She found several cans of paint of various kinds stacked in the corner, but no paintbrushes or tape. "Deah said there were close to twenty rolls of masking tape donated by a painting company."

Madison poked around in various boxes. "Look, rugby balls. There must be thirty of them."

André crossed his arms. "Someone brought them from America. Don't they know we play baseball here? Or football, the American soccer. People sometimes give us things we don't need."

A little girl wearing what looked like a floral pillowcase wandered into the room. On closer inspection, Araceli confirmed the simple dress was indeed a modified pillowcase.

Madison opened the suitcase. "Look at all these crayons. It's a wonder they don't melt in here." She fanned herself with one of the coloring books.

A box labeled "maskin tep" sat on the top shelf. Araceli was pleased to find that the label was correct—at least phonetically. "Now we can start."

"Don't you need paint, miss?" asked one of the boys who'd followed the pillowcase girl into the room.

Pulling a piece of chalk from her pocket, Araceli shook her head. "Today we are going to mark off how big the mural is and sketch out the main elements. Will you please tell the children not to rub the chalk drawings off the wall?" She left the storeroom, careful to lock the door.

André spoke to the girl, who answered him with a huge smile, then scurried out of the room.

"Marie will tell everyone to leave them alone."

The second-floor hallway and gathering area had been selected for the art gallery since the children under three lived in the first-floor nursery and dormitory and would be most likely to play with the clipboards. Araceli figured she needed eighteen inches of wall for every clipboard and frame to have enough space to not feel crowded. Currently, the orphanage housed 104 children. The building could accommodate up to 150, so she needed to plan on creating that many frames. She walked along the walls toe to heel, guesstimating the length of the hallway. Children who had materialized as if from thin air started doing the same thing, counting out loud with her. Marci had warned Araceli that she would gather a Pied Piper's–worth crowd as word spread among the children of the project.

More of the children joined in when she switched to French. *"Cinquante-deux, cinquante-trois."*

"Ninety-eleven!" shouted a boy in a blue shirt. The children around him laughed and copied him with other nonsense numbers.

Jade came around a corner and frowned. Her eyes met Araceli's, and she shook her head before returning to wherever she'd come from.

Madison rolled her eyes in Jade's direction, then joined the cacophony in a perfect German accent. *"Neunzehn, zwanzig."*

André put his hands up to stop everyone from speaking. "Hey! Hey! What are you saying, Miss Madison?"

"I am speaking German. My grandmother taught me when I was little."

André translated to the other children.

"They want to know how to speak German too."

"Yes! Please!"

"S'il vous plaît."

"Tanpri!" some begged in Haitian Creole.

When panic flashed across Madison's face, Araceli took over and directed the children in broken French to sit in a half circle in the gathering area near where they'd marked off the walls. Madison held up her index finger. *"Ein."*

"Ein."

Madison smiled and nodded. *"Zwei."*

The children mimicked her by holding up two fingers. *"Zwei."*

Araceli paced off the rest of the wall now followed only by Marie. She wondered where Tia was. She pictured the older girl from the slide presentation. If she didn't find her this morning, she would ask Marci.

Kyle hurried around the corner, followed by Jade. He stopped and studied the children, who now held up seven fingers. *"Sieben."*

The smile on Jade's face faded as Kyle went over to Araceli. "I thought you had a mini riot on your hands up here."

"No, just some enthusiastic helpers." Araceli turned and continued to heel-toe along the wall.

"What are you doing?"

"Ninety-eight," Araceli whispered before answering. "I need to know how much paintable wall there is for the art gallery before I start chalking the designs. I would hate to run out of room." Araceli took two more steps and made a mark high up on the wall.

Jade joined them. "Why did you do that?"

"I am marking every ten feet of wall."

"Why don't you use a tape measure?" Jade crossed her arms.

Araceli shrugged. "It is more fun this way. Besides, I know my tennis shoe is eleven and three-quarters inches long, and I have access to my foot whenever I need it. I won't need to go bother Tanner or Boyd every time I need to measure."

"You know your measurement won't be precise."

Araceli resisted the urge to tell Jade to put her claws away. "Of course not. This is art, not architecture."

Kyle took a half step forward, breaking the tension. "It looks like you have things in hand up here. Will you be painting today?"

"I am not sure. It depends how fast I can get things chalked off and taped." She counted off another ten steps.

"Did you find everything you needed in the donation room?"

Araceli nodded. "André was very helpful. He asked Marie to spread the word not to erase my chalk marks, so I think they'll leave them alone."

Kyle raised two fingers to his brow and gave a mock salute before heading for the central stairway. Jade narrowed her eyes for a millisecond before following him.

"I'd be careful of her if I were you," whispered Kate.

"Any idea what I did to get on her bad side?"

"You mean other than your dark curls, brown eyes, and ivory skin? She knows how to compete against all the other skinny, tan, blonde Texas socialites, but you are an enigma. And all the guys are looking at you more than they are at her."

Warmth flooded Araceli's cheeks, and she dipped her head to give the heat a moment to dissipate. "Don't worry, it won't last long. It never does." The children started clapping and counting at the same time.

"We'd better hurry up and finish." Araceli measured out the last wall. One hundred and seventy feet. She needed more. She closed her eyes and envisioned her various sketches. Staggering the clipboards was going to be her only option. But she still wanted to keep them high enough the toddlers could not easily reach the boards. "I'll be right back, I need to go grab a few of the clipboards."

Why did women feel it necessary to compete? He should have seen Jade's concern about Araceli's group for the tattletale it was. Teaching the children to count in a language they never heard was a brilliant way to entertain them. One thing the orphanage was never short on was children ready to volunteer to help any visitor, whether or not help was needed.

The roof job didn't need any young helping hands, and keeping the curious children from climbing the exterior stairway to the roof during the repair process was already tricky. It usually wasn't a problem as the children knew not to play on the roof, but the lure of watching the men remove the banks of solar panels was too great. Kyle dug through the supply room. Last fall they'd purchased three expandable gates for when they needed to move the children to the interior of the building during hurricanes as the infant and toddler rooms were all located in rooms with windows, as were the dormitories. Lack of ventilation made it necessary to keep the doors open. Last hurricane, a couple of curious toddlers had kept the workers busy in a game of escape-room junior.

Kyle moved a case of diapers and found the gates. Hopefully one at the top of the stairway would help keep the children clear of the roof area. They could still see some of the work but not be in danger.

On his way back to the roof, he passed through the third-floor common area, where Jade, Chelsea, and EmilyAnne were showing several of the teen and preteen girls how to use the sewing machines while Marci translated. His sister had started coming to the orphanage when she was only eight and picked up much of the language from her playmates. In the years since, few of them had been adopted, and the remaining ones were getting close to aging out. Marci did her best to help them find ways to further their education.

Kyle scanned the room for Marlissa. Born with cerebral palsy, the ten-year-old had been abandoned on the streets as a toddler. Marci had sponsored the child and spent most of her allowance paying for Marlissa's special education and physical therapy. She even took a job in Mom's office last summer to pay for some special braces and a speech therapist.

Some people were surprised at the fact that Marci had earned money for such a cause, but both Father and Grandfather were adamant his children and grandchildren learn to work and choose a profession. After all, it was as easy for rich kids to spend their life on the dole as it was for poor kids, and twice as easy when there was a trust fund. But waiting for the next handout was not a way to live.

Marlissa sat on the floor not far from Marci, cradling a length of pink fabric, her eyes bright with excitement. Most of the girls in the room wore similar expressions. New clothing always was cause for excitement. Kyle hoped some of them could master at least the basic sundress many of the girls wore when not in their school uniforms. Most of the dresses came from various church groups and were nothing more than pillowcases with one end cut off and ribbons attached to tie at the shoulders. The shapeless sack dresses were easy to pass down from child to child. As the girls grew, some of them felt uncomfortable in the minimal dresses and added T-shirts under them. Being able to sew dresses with proper sleeves would open their world to new fashions.

It was time to clean the outside stairs again. The birds continuously congregated under the roof—whether to escape the heat or the rain, the result was the same. A big mess.

"Martin, Wendy, come off the roof and bring the others with you, please," he called in Creole. The children who'd gathered hurried to obey. Once they were in the stairwell, Kyle put the safety gate in place. "You may watch from the stairs but no farther. *D'accord?*"

"Okay," one boy answered in the English equivalent.

A half dozen heads bobbed in agreement. "Why don't you go find a bucket and wash off all the bird droppings while you are waiting? You can each clean two steps. See if you can get it cleaned up before one of us needs to go back downstairs."

Kyle crossed the roof and joined the men from the volunteer group and a few local workers.

Boyd turned at his approach. "We are concerned about the amount of rain forecast for the week. Aselòm says it's always rainy this time of year. That is going to be a problem with the sealant. I estimate it will take at least two to three hours to dry in this humidity after the primer dries."

Kyle pulled out his phone—four bars, a rarity anyplace on the island—and checked the forecast. "It shouldn't rain again until tomorrow afternoon. Could you complete a section and then start a new area on Monday?"

"We are going to disrupt the electricity from the solar panels. If there is a power outage, they may not have enough battery power for essential areas," said Boyd.

"Can we take only part of the panels off the grid?" asked Kyle.

Boyd frowned. "I'll need to check the configuration, but I don't think so."

Kyle gestured to the city in the distance. "There is a place in Port-au-Prince we rented from in the past. We can get a couple of gas generators. That should keep the kitchen up and running if we do lose power. There are some battery-powered lanterns for the nursery area. The dormitories have windows, and there are backup batteries from the solar panels during most blackouts."

"Let's move these panels and start on the roof. With the rainy season beginning, it is better to get the roof sealed now," said Brandon.

Boyd split the men into teams. Ryan made a friendly wager involving Askanya, the famous Haitian chocolate, and the men began to work in earnest. Kyle joined a team, knowing that this was where he was most needed.

ten

AFTER LUNCH, SEVERAL OF THE children helped Madison trace the outlines of clipboards with chalk where Araceli had drawn X's on the wall. Younger children stood by observing. André grabbed a roll of masking tape and handed it to Araceli.

"We need to tape off where the boards will be mounted. No point wasting paint underneath the boards. I'll show you how, then you'll paint your own boards. You can even use the tape to make stripes and patterns."

Araceli picked at the end of the masking tape to get it started. Something was wrong. The first five inches of tape flaked off the roll. Finally, she got the tape started and pulled off about a foot, only to discover the tape wasn't sticky as it should be. She pressed a strip to the wall, but it hung limply from the one spot near the top. Rolling out another couple feet, Araceli tested it for stickiness. She rolled out several yards of tape, then tried another roll and another. Garbage—more useless than the rugby balls. Inspecting the cardboard roll, she noted the tape had been manufactured three years before she was born. The rolls must have sat in some garage someplace for over two decades for it to be this degraded.

"Okay, new plan. I need to get some tape. You help the others mark off the squares, and I'll be back." Araceli ran down the stairs and found Marci and EmilyAnne near the nursery playing clapping games with a circle of children.

Marci listened to Araceli's plight and looked at her watch. "There should be time to go get some today. I am not sure if the hardware store will be closed on Sunday or not."

"I don't want to lose another day of painting. I hoped the older children could help, and they will be in school so much of the time we are here."

"I think Kyle is up on the roof. You should ask him what he thinks."

It took a while to find the stairway leading to the roof as Araceli had walked the wrong way around the building. At the top of the stairway, she found several children vying for a spot to watch the men work. After working her way through the group, Araceli straddled the child gate, to the laughter of some of the children.

She found Kyle on the far side of the roof and showed him a scrap of the rotted tape.

"I just sent Aselòm to town on an errand. If you hurry, you might be able to catch him. He was going to stop by the kitchen first to see if we already own an adapter. Otherwise, you will have to see if we can buy some tape tomorrow or Monday. Tell him CK will have the tape."

Araceli raced back down the stairs and to the front of the orphanage. Aselòm was climbing into the SUV. She shouted for him to wait.

"I need new masking tape." Araceli held up the dried out and cracked piece. "Also some more paint brushes. Kyle said to buy tape at a place called CK."

"What kind of tape?"

"Masking—it is tan and about this wide." Araceli held her thumb and forefinger an inch apart.

"Like the blue tape the painters use?"

"Yes. Buy the tan, not blue or purple." The latter two would not work for all her needs, and there was no point getting several different kinds or widths.

The driver pursed his lips. "There are many kinds, yes? And what kind of brushes?"

As Araceli started to describe the brushes she wanted, the driver's eyes grew large. Maybe she should wait until Monday after all.

The driver nodded. "You come?"

Araceli paused. They weren't supposed to go anywhere alone, but she would be with the driver. She thought about Kyle's words. He must have assumed she would go get the things she needed herself. She should tell someone she was leaving. As Aselòm got into the driver's seat and started the car, Araceli spotted a boy who'd helped earlier and spoke understandable French.

"Manuel!"

The boy jogged over to her.

She continued in French. "Tell Miss Marci and Mr. Kyle I went to the store. D'accord?"

"D'accord, Miss Araceli. I will tell Miss Marci." Manuel ran off in the direction of the front door.

Araceli ran around to the SUV's passenger-side door, double-checking to make sure she was still wearing her fanny pack containing her money and passport. As one of the guards opened the first of the two gates for the vehicle, Araceli wondered if she should hand the two twenty-dollar bills in her pocket to Aselòm and go back. But she doubted he would bring back the type of brushes she needed. And if CK carried as many kinds of tape as some of the stores in the States did, she could end up with the wrong thing entirely. It was best to go herself.

The first coat of sealant had dried quickly, and the men now worked to spread the mesh out and fill it with the next layer of smelly black gook. Kyle knew he should have a more articulate vocabulary for the process, but construction had never interested him, even if he could follow instructions enough to be useful. Marci joined him on the roof.

"I have been listening to the radio. They are announcing blackouts for parts of Port-au-Prince area tonight and tomorrow. The nursery manager says she thinks there may be a manifestation tonight in protest."

Kyle frowned. "Boyd, how long will it take us to finish this step?"

"An hour, maybe an hour and a half. Then the sealant needs to dry at least three hours."

"Let's work as fast as we can, and hopefully the generators will be back by then. Regardless, I want all of you in the vans by four. Tonight isn't a night to be caught out on the roads. Marci, go let the other groups know they need to be packed up by four—no, make that three thirty." Jade would need to be told an earlier time. He had no idea about the rest of the group's propensity to be punctual.

Marci nodded. "No problem. I'll tell—never mind. I see the drivers are up here except for Aselòm. I was going to say I would tell the drivers."

"I sent Aselòm to get some generators. I think Araceli was asking him to get some tape too."

She stopped near the top of the stairs. "She went with him."

"She *what*?"

Several heads turned at Kyle's outburst.

"I told her to tell him what to get, not go with him."

Marci tilted her head. "Is that exactly what you said? You know sometimes you assume people understand more than you say."

Kyle pulled off his ball cap and ran his bandanna across his face. "I told her if she hurried, she could catch him. But we have been telling everyone to stick together. She should have known."

"At least it's Aselòm. He is the best driver we have ever hired. She will be safe. She isn't exactly alone."

"You are right—I hope." Kyle replaced his hat.

The inside of the car grew warm, but Aselòm told Araceli it was better she not be seen at the rental store or they would be charged double. So she slumped in her seat. Aselòm opened his door. "Do you have twenty dollars? They only have one generator left, so they raised the price. Mr. Kyle did not send enough money."

Araceli pulled one of her twenties out of her pack. Aselòm hurried off and returned ten minutes later with the generator, which he put in the back. Araceli kept her head low, hoping the store clerk would notice only her dark hair, not her pale skin. The tailgate of the SUV slammed shut, and Aselòm entered the vehicle.

"We need to hurry. That took longer than I thought. He charged me twice what he did last time we needed a generator. Remind me to tell Mr. Kyle it would be cheaper to buy one to keep on hand."

They made small talk as they drove.

"Your name—Aselòm. Does it mean something in Haitian Creole?"

The driver laughed. "Too many men."

"Too many men?"

"Yes, my parents had five boys, then me. They wanted a girl, so they named me Aselòm."

"Did it work?"

"No, they had another boy." Aselòm shook his head.

They both laughed.

They continued to one of the larger streets, perhaps the only one in the city with four distinctively painted lanes. Araceli recognized the large building visible over the wall as the American embassy, a line of people standing at the gate, hoping to get one of the elusive visas, she assumed.

The entrance to the parking lot of the CK lumberyard was a steep, man-made hill. The tall orange metal gate was rolled open. As the SUV descended into the parking lot, metal-on-metal scraping could be heard, the angle of the hill making it impossible for most vehicles to not bottom out.

"Why do they do that?"

"So cars must slow down. Harder to steal tools if you can't drive away quickly." Aselòm found a parking space, and they entered the store. Surprisingly, the store was not much different from the stores stateside. Araceli paused in the paint aisle. There was no one to mix the paint, just predetermined colors to choose from. She selected white, a green that hadn't been in the stack of colors in the storeroom, and a small can of black. A couple bags of assorted brushes would enable more children to paint at once. She also found masking tape in several sizes and styles. Araceli added six rolls to the cart. At the checkout, she was happy to find the credit card sign on the front door held true. She didn't want to spend her cash here.

At the exit, an employee checked the contents of every bag against the receipt, marking each item as he went. Not so different from an American warehouse store, only more meticulous. However, the guard with a military-style rifle slung across his shoulder glaring at them made it an experience Araceli wouldn't soon forget. She bit her lip, hoping everything had rung up correctly and not making eye contact with either the employee or the guard. When her receipt was approved, Araceli followed Aselòm to the SUV. Only when she was inside did she dare look at the guard. Shoplifting must be more of a problem than she thought.

A cloud of dust billowed on the far side of the wall, but the vehicle responsible for it moved past the orphanage. All the student volunteers were in the van. Even Jade had made it on time.

"Marci, there's a chance Aselòm will head straight for the guesthouse. Their phones must be out of range because I can't reach him or Araceli. I'll stay here. Call me if they arrive there, and have Aselòm stay the night. I can stay on the couch in the director's quarters if necessary."

"What if they come back here? Will you stay?"

"It depends. I'll call you." Kyle tipped his hat at the drivers and opened the gate for the vans. With any luck, they would be through the city before the rioting started.

eleven

THE FIVE MAKESHIFT LANES OF crawling traffic came to a stand-still on the road built for two lanes. Even the incessant honking diminished. Drivers rolled down their windows. Motorcycle taxis continued to weave into empty spaces. Aselòm turned up the air-conditioning.

Araceli looked at her phone. 4:38. "Rush hour?"

"No, Saturday all day is rush hour."

Gradually, the oncoming traffic cleared, trickling through one lane, and they inched forward like fans leaving an end-of-season Patriot's game. The smell of burning rubber filled the air. A few vehicles made U-turns and yelling men swarmed the cross street in front of them.

The driver used a few words Araceli didn't recognize, but from his tone, she figured he'd sworn in Haitian.

"What is going on?"

"It is a manifestation."

"A what?"

"They are angry at the government, so they are marching and blocking the way to the bridge. They will choose to let some cars past, then send the rest back." Aselòm looked around nervously. "I have an idea. I will lie. You must—"

A man pounded on the window. Aselòm rolled it down a few inches.

"*Vers le bas!*"

Araceli didn't need to know any French to understand the man wanted the window open wider. When Aselòm complied, the man thrust his head in, his anger evident as he glared at Araceli. He spoke to the driver in rapid Haitian Creole. Despite some words' similarity to French, she could only ascertain that the conversation revolved around her. And judging by the look on the man's face, that wasn't a positive thing.

Aselòm lifted her hand, intertwining his fingers with hers. "*Fiancée*, *green card*, and *American* became recurring words in the conversation. Weeks ago, she read a blog about Haitian men finding wives for the green card, then leaving them once they got to the States. When the conversation escalated, Aselòm gestured to the paint supplies in the back seat, then cast Araceli a tender look.

Two other men joined the first. They argued among themselves.

Aselòm took advantage of the distraction and turned to Araceli. He tapped the birthstone ring on her right hand and raised her left hand to his lips, kissing her ring finger. One of the new men bent down into the window and started to question the driver in Haitian.

Araceli slipped her ring off and moved it to the other hand.

The driver switched to French. "*Oui, elle parles français.*"

The men moved their attention to her. Her heart raced so fast she wished it could power the SUV to get them out of there. Their expressions grim, the men reminded her of the actors in TV crime dramas. The bad guys.

"How long have you known him?" the tallest one demanded.

Having no idea what answers had already been given, Araceli paused, praying for inspiration. "Long enough to know we are in love."

The man grunted, and the two behind him laughed mockingly.

"Show me your ring."

Aselòm lifted Araceli's hand, displaying the birthstone ring.

Stretching her arm to the limit, all three men took a turn inspecting the tiny cubic zirconia. Only her seat belt prevented her from being pulled onto Aselòm's lap. Never had she been so happy for an April birthday.

Apparently not satisfied, the men reverted to Haitian as they grilled the driver again.

"*Bizee elle!*" demanded one.

Araceli only had a second to register what Aselòm had been requested to do. His eyes pled for her cooperation. If only she were a better actress! She let her eyes drift closed and imitated the first movie scene that came to mind. Fueled by desperation to survive, the kiss lasted longer than most. Aselòm smiled at her before turning back to the men and speaking in Haitian again. Araceli was sure she was being called a stupid American woman, and she agreed for entirely different reasons than the context of the conversation.

The men conversed for a moment, then pointed to the gap in the blockade.

"Go!" said the man who'd required the kiss.

In French, another called, "Enjoy your honeymoon." His statement was met with laughter.

Aselòm inched the car past the roadblock. Neither of them spoke until they crossed the bridge.

"I must apologize for my lie. One of them wanted to..." Aselòm paused as if searching for the right word "...to detain you."

A shiver ran down her spine and settled in her stomach, threatening to dislodge every morsel of food she'd eaten. She closed her eyes against the nausea, glad she had not fully understood the danger. "Thank you. I am happy you lied and told him I was your stupid American green-card bride."

"You understood enough. I hoped you would. But please know I am not looking for an American bride. I have a girlfriend.

Mechelle works at the guesthouse. We are going to be married soon. She will not be happy to know I kissed you, even to save your life. But I must tell her."

"You can tell her it was like CPR."

"What means CPR?"

"It is a way to help someone to breathe and get their heart working in an emergency situation."

"Oh, I remember now. I shall use that."

The sun had sunk into the horizon when they finally turned onto the dirt road leading to the orphanage. "Mr. Kyle is not going to be very happy. We are late."

Araceli dismissed his words. Somehow, being a single white female in a car with a native after dark seemed a small danger compared to that of the past hour.

Aselòm slowed at the drainage pipe. "Stay in the car. It will scrape, but better than you walking in the dark."

Good. She wasn't sure she could walk yet.

The first gate rolled open before Aselòm could honk. Kyle stood in the center of the headlight beam, arms crossed.

"Please don't let him fire me."

The car inched forward, following Kyle and several other men to the second gate.

Araceli patted Aselòm's arm. "He won't fire you for saving my life, though he might send me back to the United States."

Thankfully the car appeared to be unscathed, the occupants unharmed. Kyle vacillated between wanting to hug both Aselòm and Araceli and shaking them both hard. A quarter hour had passed since he'd read on his phone that the police had disbanded the manifestation and cleared the roads. A dozen employees, mostly guards and kitchen workers, now crowded around them.

Aselòm got out of the car first, a look of pleading on his face. "Mr. Kyle, please don't fire me."

Araceli hurried around the car to join them. "Aselòm saved my life. You cannot let him go."

"I have no intention of firing anyone, but I am curious to know why you disobeyed the rules and went to town alone." Kyle crossed his arms and waited for an explanation.

"I did not go alone. I went with Aselòm, just as you told me to." Her voice trembled slightly.

"I told you to tell Aselòm what you needed. I never gave you permission to go into PAP." He spoke in English, knowing only about a third of those gathered would understand. Fortunately the children were in the dormitories.

"You told me to hurry so I could catch him. When I tried to explain what I needed, it was frustrating to both of us, and he said to come along. Since I wasn't alone, I figured going would be okay. I sent word." Araceli's words rushed out.

"Obviously, Miss Williams, you don't understand the gravity of what happened."

Araceli held her hand up. "What I understand is I faked being one of those American green-card brides to help get us through the roadblock. If it hadn't been for Aselòm's fast thinking, something much worse than being called a stupid woman would have happened."

Kyle stared at the ring.

As if reading his mind, Araceli moved the ring to her other hand, both hands shaking. "Obviously we suffered a major miscommunication, and I'll understand if you want to put me on the next flight out of here. But whatever you decide, Aselòm should not be blamed for any of this."

He kept his gaze on the ring. "You could have been seriously injured or—"

Araceli shoved her shaking hands in her pockets, but the rest of her continued to shiver. It may have been the mix of the headlights and the light cast from the lamps, but she looked paler than she did a moment ago.

Shock.

He'd seen the warning signs often enough during counseling and had avoided pushing patients too far. How had he missed them? The slight sheen of sweat on her face wasn't from anger or defensiveness or even the humidity, as he'd assumed. He needed to get her lying down, or at least sitting, before she fainted. "You both look like you can use some water. Come into the office while the director sets up the generators." Kyle held out his hand, but Araceli didn't move.

"There is only one generator. They didn't have any more and charged me double for the one."

Kyle nodded to Aselòm and replied in Haitian. "You were lucky to get it. The city announced the planned blackouts shortly after you left."

The driver headed for the rear of the SUV.

"Aselòm, let the others set the generator up while you get something to eat."

Kyle reached for Araceli's elbow. Thankfully she didn't fight him as he led her to the door at the side of the porch and into the office. The single light bulb did little to illuminate the corners of the room. At his guidance, Araceli sat on the worn couch. Kyle pulled up a folding chair and sat opposite her.

"Do you feel like you are going to faint?"

Slowly she shook her head. "Not anymore. Thanks for finding me a place to sit."

She leaned back and closed her eyes. After a few minutes, her breathing evened out, and she quit shaking. Kyle went over to one of the high cupboards and unlocked it. A bottle of water, albeit warm, and a granola bar would help. He also grabbed a small bag of fruit snacks before relocking the cupboard. He handed them to Araceli. "Not the best dinner, but it will help to keep you from fainting."

She unscrewed the water bottle cap and took a long drink. "Why do you have food locked up in here?"

"So the little monkeys won't run off with it. I also council incoming children, transitioning children, and prospective adoptive parents. Sometimes I find having a snack on hand helps the situation. But treats like the fruit snacks are not a daily occurrence for the children here, so I lock them up." Kyle sat back down in the folding chair. "So, what happened at the manifestation?"

Between bites, Araceli described the mob scene and Aselòm's ruse. "It wasn't until we were almost here that I realized how much danger I was in. If the men had taken me from the car, at the very least they would have used me as a punching bag. I guess I lost it for a moment out there."

Kyle ripped open the fruit snacks and extended the bag to her. "If you are referring to near fainting, you didn't lose it, because that is a perfectly normal reaction to the type of emotional trauma you experienced. If you are talking about yelling back at me, that isn't losing it, either."

"Are you going to send me back?" A puppy dog's brown eyes couldn't have pled her case any better than Araceli's did.

"Normally, maybe. But Marci did point out I may not have been very explicit in my instructions, making this partially my fault. I think if you leave after what happened today, it will only give you nightmares of the country I love, and I want you to see the good here. Do you want to stay?"

"Very much. I should have thought through my actions better. Please don't fire Aselòm."

"Aselòm is one of my favorite drivers. Some might not have tried to protect you or even the SUV. I don't want to scare you further, but had you been with another driver, it could have been worse than being alone. I suppose we need to be clearer in the future that going off alone means taking another one of the volunteers with you. Although, in this case, if you had taken a second volunteer, I am not sure what tale Aselòm could have spun to diffuse the situation."

"What do we do now?"

"It's best if we go back to the guesthouse. The orphanage is not equipped for overnight guests, and there is already speculation among the workers as to what happened tonight." Kyle didn't add that Araceli flashing her ring may have added fuel to the poorly translated conversation. "I'll go see if one of the other drivers can take us to the guesthouse in a different vehicle."

twelve

THE CREAKING BUNK BEDS AND the click-clack of the fan woke Araceli. EmilyAnne, fresh from the shower, wore a towel wrapped around her head, her flip-flops slapping a rhythm against the tile floor proclaiming "Wake-up, wake-up!" Araceli sat up and moved the mosquito netting out of the way.

Marci hopped down from the top bunk. "How did you sleep? I was caught with my Mom and Dad in a manifestation a couple years ago. Our driver lied and said we were expected back at the embassy, implying we were in charge of getting more funds from the government. I don't think I slept well for two weeks."

"I didn't have any nightmares." But she'd hardly slept. Between the images floating in front of her eyes, the stupid mosquito that had found his way inside of the netting, and a rooster who thought it was an alarm clock, there hadn't been time for nightmares.

Jade shook out a lavender shirt and matching capris. "So, when is your flight?"

"What flight?" Araceli paused, unzipping her case.

"Back to Illinois or wherever you're from. I'm surprised Kyle even brought you back to the guesthouse instead of dropping you off at the airport."

Madison pulled a pair of socks on. "Weren't you there when they got back last night? Kyle said he wasn't sending her home because the misunderstanding was partially his fault."

"But she still should have known being with a driver was the same as leaving alone. She put others in danger." Jade put her hand on her hip and glared at Araceli.

Araceli slipped into the bathroom, leaving the conversation behind. Getting into a fight with Jade would serve no purpose and might get her sent back after all. Kyle may have been kind last night, but that kindness didn't change the fact he was put out with her. After the forty-minute drive back to the guesthouse, his terse explanation to the group playing card games around the kitchen table had left even Marci staring in shock.

No one dared leave the orphanage compound without explicit instructions for the rest of this trip.

Araceli made quick work of her shower and twisted her hair into a messy bun. The rest of the women had gone down to breakfast before she emerged from the bathroom. As she sat on the edge of her bed to change her flip-flops for shoes and socks, the sound of crumpling paper startled her.

She moved to the side and found a note written on a torn piece of paper. She recognized only a few words. Bringing up her Haitian Creole dictionary on her phone, she began to translate. By the time she'd read the second line, it was evident the author meant to insult her using words she wouldn't repeat in English. The third line even contained a possible death threat. Araceli bit her lip. Her misspelled name at the top of the page left no doubt that the placement on her bed was not a mistake. Should she show the note to Marci? Would the teen even know the words she'd looked up on her phone?

She was walking into the hallway, studying the paper in her hand, when a wall stopped her progress and the paper fluttered to the floor. Not a wall—Kyle. He bent to pick up the paper before she could.

As he read the note, his eyes widened. "Where did you get this?"

"It was on my bed."

Kyle studied her as if trying to read her thoughts. "How much of this do you understand?"

"Enough to be more than slightly shaken." Araceli tried to smile.

"Have you eaten breakfast?"

She shook her head. "I was going down."

"Bring your food up here to the terrace. We need to talk." Kyle opened the door leading to the empty terrace.

A private breakfast with Kyle wasn't going to make her morning any better. Although she'd lost her appetite, Araceli hurried to get a plate of food. She didn't dare disobey him.

Marci was the only other American besides Mrs. Delino, the guesthouse owner, with enough knowledge of Haitian to have written the note. However, the handwriting didn't belong to either woman. Kyle suspected it must be Aselòm's girlfriend, Mechelle, who had written it. Yet the venom spewed across the page did not seem in proportion to what he knew of the driver's ruse yesterday to get them safely out of the manifestation. Had Aselòm and Araceli left something out of their story?

He'd heard Mrs. Delino tell her story of marrying a Haitian and choosing to stay. As a white female, she'd suffered a number of threats and rumors, some of which had been life-threatening, before she married.

He knew the threats on the paper in his hand were not entirely idle. And since Mechelle worked here at the guesthouse, she would have the means to carry out any number of unpleasant retaliations.

The door to the terrace opened, and Araceli stepped onto the porch, balancing a plate on top of her juice glass. Kyle stood from the table and pulled out a chair opposite him. "I need to know if something else happened during the manifestation yesterday other than you switching your ring from one hand to the other."

Araceli used her fork to move the scrambled eggs around her plate, not looking up as she answered. "They told us to kiss."

Aselòm must've given his girlfriend a more detailed version of the story than Kyle received. "I take it you obeyed their direction."

Araceli did not look up, but he could see the pink that flooded her face. "It seemed like the best thing to do at the moment."

"Most likely it was." A tiny jealous monster somewhere in Kyle's brain gave out a little whine. At least she didn't seem the type who ran around kissing every guy who asked. "I'm going to assume Aselòm told Mechelle about the kiss when he was trying to explain the encounter. I can't speak for all Haitian women, but I have heard stories before of over-the-top jealousy. We need her to see and understand that whatever happened in the car during the manifestation was done to safely extract yourselves from the situation."

Araceli continued playing with her food.

"You really should eat."

"I seem to have lost most of my appetite."

Wanting to reassure her, he said, "You didn't do anything wrong. You just managed to get yourself in a bit of a mess."

"How am I supposed to get myself out?"

Kyle leaned back in his chair and swirled the last of his mango juice in his cup. "I have an idea you probably aren't going to like, but hear me out. If we can show Aselòm's girlfriend you are in a relationship with another man and have no designs on Aselòm, I think she will back off."

"So you're telling me I need to choose one of the guys and pretend to be his girlfriend for the rest of the trip?"

"Pretty much. But not just one of the guys. Me."

"I can't do that." Araceli pushed back from the table and walked over to the wrought-iron railing overlooking the yard.

Kyle followed her. "Why not?"

She studied the tall palm trees in the yard, not turning toward him. "I'm not that great of an actress."

"You must've done a convincing job yesterday."

She blushed again. "It was only for a few minutes. And I just pretended to be a famous actress. You're asking me to pretend to be your girlfriend for a whole week, and I don't know how to be that person."

"Be my girlfriend? Or anyone's girlfriend?"

Araceli finally turned to look at him. "Both, I guess. I spent most of my life disliking you. It took me years to shed that stupid nickname, and my older brother still calls me by it sometimes when he is teasing me and he is married now. I haven't had much experience with the real-girlfriend thing to even know what to fake."

He cupped her elbow. "I hadn't thought of the name I called you until the other day when I saw you on the plane. I hoped you had forgotten. I owe you a long-overdue apology, but there really hasn't been a moment to give it. Can you forgive me for being a stupid fourteen-year-old boy?"

"My brother's friends overheard you calling me Celi-Belly and teased me with the stupid song for the next three years. Not until I started running track and they'd graduated from high school did the nickname die." Her eyes glistened with unshed tears.

One spilled over.

Kyle reached over to wipe it away with his thumb. "I had no idea I hurt you so much. Can you forgive me?" He resisted the urge to pull her into his arms to try to erase everything with a hug.

Araceli turned away and started searching her pockets. Kyle pulled a clean tissue out of his own pocket and handed it to her.

"I can forgive you. But I can't play Meg Ryan to your Tom Hanks or Emma Stone to your Ryan Gosling. I'm not saying—" Araceli waved her hands as if they could help her search for words. "I'm not saying I don't find you attractive. I'm saying I don't know how to pretend a relationship for a week."

Kyle's heart sped up at her admission. What if? "It shouldn't be too hard. Most of the time we'll be with other people and fairly busy. We need to take the time to talk and perhaps hold hands when we are together. And perhaps a kiss or two for show." He stepped closer.

She didn't back away, but she lowered her eyes. "I'm not very good at physical stuff."

"Kissing? You must have been yesterday."

"That was because my life depended on it. I was trying to imitate every kiss I'd ever seen in every rom-com I've ever watched. I was so afraid if I did the kiss wrong, they would hurt us."

Interesting. Kyle tried to add up what she was telling him. He couldn't believe she hadn't had much experience as a girlfriend or being kissed. However, asking her such a thing point-blank would hardly break down her defenses. "We could try fake dating for a couple of days. If it doesn't work, you can slap me someplace where we will be seen and make sure you avoid Aselòm."

"They'll think I am some sort of loose woman. That won't help, will it?"

Kyle shook his head. "I don't think anyone who has spoken to you or looked into your eyes would ever think you are a loose woman."

She blinked and raised her gaze to meet his. The tears were gone, replaced by a wariness. "When this is over, can we part as friends?"

Kyle gently ran his hand down her cheek. "I hope so." He moved his gaze to her lips, then back to her eyes.

Araceli gave the slightest of nods, her eyes imitating his movements.

Kyle slid his hand down and lifted her chin.

Araceli froze.

"I promise I don't bite." Kyle kept the kiss light and pulled back before his instincts could overrule his mind.

She was blushing.

He kissed her again. This time she kissed him back.

"There you are!" Jade's interruption ripped them apart.

Araceli's burning cheeks had nothing to do with the sun warming the patio. Keeping her back to Jade, she willed the flames to die down—at least the ones in her cheeks. Araceli had no idea what to do with the other things she was feeling. It was supposed to be a fake kiss. Someone needed to tell that to her heart so it would slow down. Kyle's hand slid down her arm and found her hand. He gave her fingers a little squeeze that sent tingles up her arm.

"Did you need something, Jade?"

"Aselòm called the house line. The drivers should be here in fifteen minutes."

Araceli turned to face Jade. There was no point in hiding. Jade's smirk matched the one Araceli's imagination had conjured up. "Let the gossip begin." Araceli said under her breath, hoping only Kyle could hear her.

Kyle whispered in her ear. "In three, two, one."

Jade whirled from the patio and went back into the house.

"You'd better finish your breakfast. We have a full day in front of us. Besides, you won't get better mangos than the ones the Delinos find for us."

Kyle led Araceli back to her meal. She was surprised to find her appetite had returned.

"I don't want you in whatever vehicle Aselòm is driving. And I am sorry to say, the rides are probably going to be the hardest part of this. You'll have to pretend to like me for almost a solid hour."

"I think I can do that." Araceli finished the last couple of bites.

He reached for her dishes. "I'll take them down. You finish getting ready and don't forget to brush with bottled water."

Oh, ratzelfratzel! Araceli had just experienced the best kiss of her life with morning breath!

The drive to the orphanage flew by for Kyle, partially due to the lazy Sunday morning traffic but mostly because of Araceli's company. They sat in the back of one of the vans with Madison.

Although Madison raised a brow at Araceli when she must have thought he wasn't looking, she kept her comments to herself. Mercifully, Jade was in the other van. Only Marci cast him questioning looks. Kyle debated about telling Marci the truth, but even one whisper would threaten their plan. He needed to warn Araceli about his sister's tenacious nature.

"Is that really all garbage?" Madison pointed out the window.

"Sadly, yes," Marci responded from the front seat.

"They are selling food there." Ryan sounded horrified.

"This is one of the reasons we caution you against buying food from street vendors." Kyle watched Araceli as he spoke and drew little designs on the back of her hand with his thumb. They'd only kissed an hour ago, and his body was already telling him how impossible faking would be with this woman.

thirteen

THE VOLUNTEERS WORKED QUICKLY AND quietly to prepare the surprise. Taking one hundred children to church was not an option since the orphanage didn't own any school buses of their own. So each Sunday a devotional was held in the upstairs schoolroom, led by the director and his wife. The words to a popular children's hymn crescendoed above them. Araceli recognized the tune but not the words, so she assumed they were singing in Haitian Creole. Marci told the volunteers when they heard that song play they had only about five minutes left to prepare.

Araceli hurried to scatter the last of her Easter eggs. Last night before she'd returned to the orphanage, the others had filled the cardboard eggs with stickers and candy. Made from painted toilet-paper tubes pinched closed at each end, the easily transportable and biodegradable eggs would serve their purpose. Now, five hundred eggs lay scattered in sections around the orphanage.

Shouts came through the building as the meeting ended and the children rushed downstairs for the annual hunt. The older children helped the younger ones get into groups by age, then Marci explained the rules. Araceli didn't understand the words but could tell from the counting and recounting of fingers on one hand that the limit was five eggs. Workers and volunteers were sent out to each section to supervise.

Marci counted to five again, then whistled, and the children scattered. She took a little girl by the hand and led her to a smaller area where Kyle stood. Araceli watched as he tapped near the eggs with his foot. After a moment, she realized the child was blind and that there was a bell in each egg.

Shouting from nearby claimed her attention.

One boy had gathered an armful of eggs. Araceli hunched down to eye level and held her hand up, counting each finger in French and pointing at the boy's arms. Downcast, the boy dropped most of his eggs to the ground, and the other children snatched them up.

When they were finished, the children gathered around the porch and compared finds. Boys and girls traded stickers, hoping to find their favorites.

Araceli walked around the perimeter to Kyle's side. "Do you do this every year?"

"This is the fourth year. Marci's idea. Bringing five hundred plastic eggs to Haiti wasn't practical, so she came up with the idea of using toilet-paper tubes. I think half her high school saves them for her. And each year she holds a huge painting party."

"The little girl who searched on her own—is she blind?"

"Yes."

"I didn't even notice yesterday, and I know I saw her running around with the other toddlers."

"Despite few resources, she has learned to cope. Where we can, we adapt things for her. She has no problem navigating the bottom floor of the orphanage. Like the rest of the two-year-olds, we try to keep her on the main floor."

Araceli studied the toddler as she opened her eggs. Instead of stickers, there were pompoms and foam letters inside. "What are her prospects here?"

"Probably what you assume. There is one school for the blind in Port-au-Prince. Fortunately, she is in the adoption process. Her adoptive parents have been working on learning Haitian, and some of the oldest children work with her each day to learn English. We are hopeful everything will be complete by this fall so she can get into American schools."

"She is under three. Did the process get fast-tracked?"

"The adoptive family fell in love with her when she was less than six months old. They have been very persistent in their petitions. It helps that the mother-to-be is a special-education teacher. For once the government officials agree that a fast adoption, meaning less than two years, is in the best interest of everyone."

"How long is a slow adoption?"

"The average adoption takes about four years. That's why when a child reaches fourteen we shift focus to prepare them to live on their own once they age out."

"Wow, that must make the high school years rough."

"You have no idea." Kyle took Araceli's hand and led her around the edge of the group to the door that went directly into the office.

Only twelve hours ago she'd stood in this same room, heart racing, wondering how fast he would send her home. "What are we doing in here?" He wouldn't take advantage of their arrangement, would he? Most guys would. How far would he push it? If only she could talk to her roommates! Candace would have a ton of advice for her, but would she have a phone at a living-history thing? No way would she bug Tessa and Sean. Tessa already had too much to wrap her mind around, falling in love and then finding out Sean had inherited more than a billion dollars.

Kyle touched her arm. "Hey, don't look so scared. I thought I'd give everyone out there something to speculate about, but that doesn't mean I'm going to take advantage of you."

"I'm not sure I really want to be speculated about." It was the opening she'd waited for to ask what she wanted to know since their kiss. "So, on the terrace—you knew Jade was watching?"

Kyle leaned back on his desk, putting his eyes level with hers. "I was fairly sure someone was, but I also needed to know if we could pull this off. If the chemistry was real. If you had forgiven me."

"Oh. And this?" Araceli indicated the closed door.

"If we don't spend at least some time alone, it's not going to make people believe. Just so you know, Aselòm's girlfriend's sister works in the kitchens here."

"Thanks for the heads-up. Now, if you don't mind, I think we've spent enough time alone to raise an eyebrow or two. I'm going to go gather my group and start painting."

Kyle took a seat at his desk. "I'll see you later."

She waved before exiting, biting her lip to keep from saying the first words crossing her mind: *"Looking forward to it."*

It didn't take long for Marci to corner him in the office.

"So, is it true?" She crossed her arms and leaned against the door, preventing his escape.

"Is what true?"

"Did Jade really catch you making out on the terrace?"

"I don't know that the kiss she witnessed qualifies for making out."

Marci's jaw dropped. "I don't believe it. You have known Araceli less than three days."

"More like fourteen years. Her brother is Greg. He has come to visit a few times."

"I know that, but I was, like, four when you met her, and I know she has never visited. Nor have you ever spoken. So that doesn't count. So spill it. Kyle Evans doesn't go around kissing random women."

"I don't know that I want to discuss my love life with you, squirt." Kyle moved to open the door.

Marci refused to budge.

"I need to go help on the roof. I assume you are helping some-place." Kyle picked her up and moved her to the side.

"Fine. I'll ask Araceli."

"Leave her alone."

"Oh, you're protective of her!" Marci clapped her hands with glee and exited the room.

Kyle took the long way through the building so he could check on the sewing and painting projects.

A couple of the older teens, including Tia, had finished their dresses and were modeling them, the smiles on their faces worth more than any haute-couture dress on Madison Avenue. The other children celebrated for them.

Chelsea looked up and elbowed Jade when they caught sight of him. He had not accounted for Jade when he'd come up with his plan to protect Araceli. She was subtler than a spurned Haitian woman but perhaps just as dangerous. It didn't help that she had openly flirted with him for the past three years.

Tia ran up to him, speaking rapidly in Haitian Creole. "Mr. Kyle! Isn't this the best dress in the world? And I made it! I am going to help Marlissa with hers, only hers will be yellow." Marlissa stood nearby clutching a length of flowered fabric.

"I think her dress will be gorgeous too." It was nice to see Tia excited about something. The first weeks after arriving, she'd resembled a zombie more than a child.

Marci stood at the cutting table, where she translated directions. All the volunteers appeared to be engaged with the children, and none of the children looked to be ignored.

Kyle took the ramp up to the second floor where several chil-dren worked at taping the walls of the hallway with the new masking tape. He found Araceli in the open classroom helping children paint their initials on the corner of the clipboards. He laid his hand on her back and waited for her to finish speaking. When she turned to him, he took her hand and led her out to the hallway.

"I need to warn you to watch out for my sister and Jade."

Araceli made no move to remove her hand from his. "Marci?"

"She is tenacious and not always discreet. She's more than a little concerned I kissed you after so short of an acquaintance." Kyle hoped he wasn't blushing. He didn't want to admit to Araceli that she was the first woman he had kissed or even wanted to kiss in quite a while. "I think it best she keeps pondering."

"How much trouble will Jade cause?"

Kyle shrugged. "I don't know. She has been ingratiating herself with my mother and Cassie for two years. But she isn't ..." *Nice, creative ... you.* "She isn't ..."

"Okay, so Aselòm's girlfriend will cut holes in my mosquito netting, and Jade will short-sheet my bed?" Araceli smiled up at him.

"I'm afraid Jade will be subtler than that." Kyle gave her hand a squeeze. "I'll see you later."

Araceli slipped back into the classroom.

Kyle found himself smiling all the way to the roof, where everyone worked in earnest to race the afternoon storm.

André helped Araceli write the names of each child in the taped squares. They placed a *C* on all the frames corresponding with children under age five and an *E* every five squares or so to match the empty beds in the orphanage. Any child over the age of five who wanted the opportunity to help paint their own frame could do so.

The younger children who didn't go to school would help with the handprint animals that would be painted in the nursery hallway later that week.

Madison and EmilyAnne helped the children decorate their clipboards in groups of ten.

The crowd of children watching dwindled as the day continued. Araceli walked around to see that everyone was engaged before picking up a box of chalk. This was the only part of the project where she hadn't figured out how to have the children do most of the work. As fast as she could, she created decorative picture frames around each taped off square. Attempting to make each of the dozens of frames unique complicated the process. Art Deco to Dr. Seuss, traditional to rococo. After the first forty, her arm began to droop.

EmilyAnne came out of the classroom. "I think we have finished with all the boards for the four- to seventeen-year-olds. There are definitely a few artists in here. I wrote down their names so you can recruit them after school next week."

It was harder to read the paper than it should have been. Araceli looked for a light switch before remembering this was one of the rooms that relied on daylight from several large windows. Heavy clouds covered the sky. She wondered if the men had reached a point on the roof where they could stop without the rain ruining everything they had done.

Earlier that morning while retrieving the new tape from the storeroom, she'd noticed a pile of tarps and heavy plastic drop cloths. Perhaps they could be used to protect the roof. "André, quick! Get some of the boys and come to the storeroom."

They reached the child gate at the top of the outside stairway just as the first droplets fell from the sky.

"Kyle, Tanner, Boyd!" she yelled to get the attention of the men.

Boyd jogged over. "Where did you find these? We were wishing we had purchased some." He took a folded tarp from one of the boys and passed it to Tanner.

"They were in the storeroom with the paint."

Kyle reached for the drop cloths she carried. "Good thinking." His hand brushed hers, for a second the rain, men, and children faded into the background.

When the connection broke, Araceli was left with one thought. The acting felt far too real.

According to Boyd, if they could keep the rain off the section of the roof they'd sealed for another half hour, it would be cured. They stretched tarps between the solar panels they'd remounted where they finished yesterday and the still-unsealed roof. Racing to beat the real downpour, Boyd yelled instructions, some of them seeming to counter to what Kyle would have done, but once the tarps were tied down, it was evident Boyd had seen a bigger design from the beginning.

As they all moved back to check their work, Kyle stepped in a puddle where the water pooled near the edge of the newly completed section.

"Hey, is this going to be a problem?" Kyle pointed to the water around his foot.

Boyd muttered a word Kyle hoped none of the children heard, grabbed some of the remaining drop cloths, and instructed the others to do the same. "Roll them up like sausages!" In minutes, a makeshift dam had channeled the water toward another rain spout.

As the raindrops multiplied, the men took shelter in the enclosed stairwell.

Boyd looked at his watch. "Come on! Fifteen more minutes!" he yelled at the sky.

Tanner put his arm on Boyd's shoulder. "Nothing you can do now. We have to wait it out, then check on it."

"Worst case, we should only have to redo one coat," said Brandon. "At least Kyle's girlfriend thought of bringing those tarps up."

"She's n—" Kyle thought better of the denial on his lips. Tanner's raised brow begged him to finish the sentence. "She's nice and thoughtful that way."

"Thought you were going to tell us she wasn't your girlfriend. Which would be nice because I would love to take a turn kissing her too."

"Too?"

"First the driver, then you. She didn't look like that kind of a girl, but..." Tanner wisely trailed off.

Kyle counted to five before answering. "Araceli is *not* that kind of girl. I don't know what you heard about what happened with the driver, but if she had not kissed Aselòm as those thugs at the manifestation requested, there is a very real chance she could be in the hospital today. As for kissing me, that is between the two of us."

Tanner held up his hands. "Backing off. My bad. I guess I didn't understand the full situation when I heard the other drivers talking."

"I can't keep watching this. Let's go see what we can do inside, like measure the director's kitchen." Boyd headed downstairs, the others following behind him.

As they hurried down the stairs to the staccato beat of the falling rain, Kyle glared at the back of Tanner's head. He couldn't remember the last time he wanted to punch someone over a woman.

They'd finished measuring the counter when the lights flickered twice and went out. Kyle glared at the single bulb overhead. "Y'all better pack it up. Unlikely they will get power back today, and we don't want to drain any extra resources. I'll meet you down at the vans."

Even on the brightest of days, many of the areas on the third floor were cast in shadow. Kyle narrowly avoided running into a couple of boys who had been playing with cars in one of the unused rooms. "Come downstairs. It's almost dinnertime."

"No, it's not Mr. Kyle. You know we got at least two hours, and with the power out, it won't be no good anyway."

"*Any* good," Kyle automatically corrected. "And we have a generator, so the ovens will still work."

The boys parked their cars in the corner and followed him downstairs. Marci held a battery-powered lantern at the entrance of the storeroom. Kate and Madison set their paint cans back on the shelves, and Araceli supervised the cleaning up in French.

"Please put all the brushes in here." She held a plastic bin full of murky water.

"I hope you aren't planning on washing those." Kyle spoke in French, knowing every child over ten understood them and wouldn't wonder what was being said.

"No, I understand that when the power goes out the water doesn't always work, and they don't like using the cistern unless it's an emergency. The paint is water based. Keeping the brushes wet will work until a better time to clean them arises."

"I see you thought of everything."

"Your mother did."

"Do you need anything?"

Araceli shook her head and turned her attention to a boy who had as much paint on his hands as his brush.

Instead of taking the stairs, Kyle used the ramp to the main floor. The sewing area was nearly clean. Several other girls wore new dresses. "Jade, do you need anything?"

"We need to store the machines in one of the offices."

"Let's put them in the one I use." He pulled the key ring from his pocket and picked up two of the sewing machines by their handles. Jade followed him down the dimly lit hallway. With the blinds closed, the office was dark. "Please keep the door propped open while I put these away, and then I'll get yours."

As Kyle set the second sewing machine next to the first, he heard the door shut behind him. He turned and tried to see in the darkened room. He pulled the phone out of his pocket. "Jade?"

The dim light of his phone revealed that she was only inches away. She placed her right hand on his chest. "What does Miss Artist have that I don't? I've been coming on these trips for years. I understand your family. I know what you need. According to Cassie, you didn't even think a mural was a viable project. I hear she is free with her favors. Is that it? Was I playing too hard to get?" Jade reached for his phone, her fingers covering his as she turned it off, her lips covered his before he had time to react. They tasted of artificial strawberries, the heavy coating of gloss slithering along his lips. He pulled away, but she tried again, this time finding his neck.

"Jade, stop this." He took her by both shoulders and held her at a distance. "I've never had anything but a friendship with you. I thought you understood this years ago."

"No! No, I don't understand." She found the exterior door outlined faintly by the closed blinds and rushed out.

Kyle leaned against his desk and rubbed his temples. Only two days in and his biggest headache was women.

fourteen

THE GRAY LIGHT FILTERING THROUGH the rain beckoned Araceli to the outside door, where she found Jade blocking her exit from the building. "Kyle will never be yours. Go back to Podunk Indiana or wherever you're from!" Jade's smudged lipstick twisted the hard-edged words.

If a Picasso could speak, it would look just like Jade. The absurd thought nearly made Araceli laugh. The angry girl pushed past Araceli and went back into the building. Most of the volunteers stood about the patio watching the rain. Kyle was not among them. On the far side of the patio, his office door stood ajar.

She entered. "Do you have a headache?"

Kyle lifted his head. The other half of the Picasso. The not-so-funny half. Araceli turned, hoping Kyle hadn't seen her reaction. They were fake dating, so the heaviness she felt in her stomach should be fake too.

A hand on her elbow stopped her. "Hey, what's wrong?"

She turned to face him. "That shade of lipstick clashes with your—"

"Oh!" Kyle pulled a tissue from his pocket and rubbed his face, farther smearing ruby red. "This isn't what it looks like."

"I am not your real girlfriend, so it doesn't matter what lipstick all over your face looks like to me. Just others. And considering Jade's lipstick is also smeared across her face, I suggest we clean you up." Araceli dug for a baby wipe in her pack, then ran it with more pressure than necessary across his face. She folded the wipe before erasing the trail of red kisses on the side of his neck. Where skin met cotton, she stopped. "Next time, I suggest you ask her to wear less lipstick. Getting the stain out of clothing is a pain."

"Celi—"

"Araceli."

"Look, I didn't kiss her."

"The evidence says otherwise. I don't know what game you like to play with your volunteers, but I don't want to be part of it. I'll take my chances of having someone destroy my mosquito netting rather than becoming some pawn or conquest for you."

"Please—"

It was the same please Wesley must have given the Dread Pirate Roberts in her favorite book. She sighed. "I'll listen."

"I was helping Jade put the sewing machines away. It was dark in here, and I literally didn't see her coming. She has danced this same dance with me for years. It has never been more than friendship, and after today it may not be even that. I know what we are doing isn't, well...you know, but I am not the type of guy who goes around making pawns of people or conquests of women. I was honest about what we agreed to this morning. You are not a number, and I hope you are my friend."

She wasn't sure when he had taken her hands in his during the speech, the gentle warmth radiating from them melting her insides. If he did want to manipulate her, he had the perfect weapons. Remembering their relationship was fake was easier than believing it was real. She pulled her hands out of his. "So how do we play this? Do I act like I have forgiven you or I don't know?"

"What do you want to do?"

Slap Jade. Slap you, maybe. Kiss you. The last thought had to be a mistake. "We should probably join the others. And let's keep our relationship to holding hands for now." People may assume something more anyway, and it was safer for her heart.

"Let me make sure this room is locked." He retook her hand as they stepped back on the porch.

Araceli wished she liked his touch a bit less.

Kyle counted heads. Where was Jade? He'd turned to ask Marci to go find her when Jade walked out of the building, makeup fixed and chin held high. She marched past him and into one of the vans. The van he was supposed to be in. Of course, she took the last remaining seat—the one next to Araceli.

"Jade, Chelsea is in the other van holding a seat for you."

"Oh, this is fine. You can go in the other van."

"Marci is in the other van, and we need a Haitian speaker in this one. Just in case we run into another manifestation. Tensions are still high, and with another power outage…" Tensions were high, and his blood pressure was spiking.

"Make someone else move, like Articili here."

"Her name is Araceli, and you were the last one out. Please go get in the other van."

Boyd opened the door to the front-passenger seat. "Here, dude, I'll move."

"Thanks."

"Good luck," Boyd whispered as he passed Kyle.

Kyle climbed in and glanced back to where Araceli sat next to Jade. Side by side, it was easy to make comparisons. Where Jade looked like she had walked out of a fashion magazine, one of those that put models in the faux real-life situations, Araceli looked relaxed and prepared. Her clothes were neither new nor very old, and she didn't seem to mind having paint on them.

Spirals of hair poked out from her messy bun. She watched out the window the same way she watched everything else, including him—as if she were studying and learning. Jade watched people too, but only to see who was watching her.

As they started to turn the first corner, the driver stopped. The rain had washed another section of soil away near the large pipe. "Everyone must walk, or I not get van over." The driver's English was not as clear as Aselòm's.

Kyle hopped out and opened the rear door to the van. "Come on, y'all. I know it's raining, so let's hurry." He looked sternly at Jade, daring her to argue. She glared but got out, the passengers in the other van were getting out as well.

"Tomorrow I'll come out here and look at what we can do to fill this. I noticed some brick builders near the bridge. Would the locals have left a few cobblestones behind?" asked Tanner.

"Maybe we can get some broken pavers that haven't been appropriated for another use." Kyle followed the others down the road to where the vans now waited.

Jade climbed back into the van after Araceli. This was not going to be a fun ride. In the time it had taken to drive the mile or so to the paved road, the dirt road had become a small river. Kyle was grateful they'd left when they did. The runoff would have prevented their exit if it had risen much higher.

The occupants of the van were strangely quiet. Rain often had that effect on people—perhaps it was the origin of the phrase "dampened spirits." The traffic moved slowly as usual, although there were fewer moto taxis. The advantage of no traffic lights was that they couldn't go out to cause further problems with the power outage.

Thirty minutes into the drive, Marci texted him. **Boyd asked about the lights over in Pétion-Ville. Can we rearrange things and go this afternoon?**

Good idea. I'll phone the guesthouse. I don't think they will have started on dinner yet.

Kyle spoke to the driver in Haitian as he dialed the guesthouse. "Do you mind driving to Pétion-Ville?"

"No problem."

Mrs. Delino answered on the third ring. Kyle explained the change of plans.

"Since I didn't make it to the market before the storm hit, I am pleased. Without your group, I will have enough food to serve the others."

Kyle texted Marci back. **Good to go.**

See you there.

Kyle turned to face the rest of the passengers. "We are taking advantage of our early end to the day to take a drive through Pétion-Ville, where we will also stop for dinner."

Jade clapped her hands. "Pétion-Ville is one of my favorite parts of the trip. Shopping!"

"We will have to go souvenir shopping another day. With the rain, most of the street artists will have closed shop. We won't be stopping at Rivoli as that store is closed on Sunday, and you don't need another Rolex for your father. We will stop for dinner."

They meandered up the hill into what was perhaps the most prosperous area of Haiti.

"Whoa, a stoplight. I didn't think those existed here," Tanner said from the back seat.

The driver glanced in the rearview mirror. "This week the light is not working. It shows red to both sides. So we take turns."

"It wasn't working last year either." Jade leaned into Araceli, trying to see out the window.

Kyle resumed his role as tour guide. "Pétion-Ville is home to several embassies, and foreign dignitaries tend to choose to live there. It isn't as exclusive as Labadee, but still, most everything sold in Pétion-Ville is out of reach for the average Haitian."

"Where is Labadee?" Araceli didn't look away from the window as she asked.

"Labadee is on the north part of the island. It is meant for tourists only. Although locals work there, they don't live there. The cruise ships dock there. Many tourists claim to have been to Haiti, but they only see the facade that is Labadee. No cinder-block huts and no beggars. Like Pétion-Ville, you can find many street artists in Labadee."

"Are we going there on this trip?"

"Probably not. I need to go to Jacmel, in the opposite direction."

Jade stuck out her lower lip.

Maybe Kyle would find a way to go to Jacmel without Jade.

The driver wound through streets, passing several embassies and European-style churches. Kyle was content to follow the van Marci directed, knowing she would hit all the highlights. No doubt her tour was better than his. They stopped at a midrange restaurant featuring local Haitian bands and music.

Kyle managed to sit next to Araceli. Her hair hung free of the bun. If they were genuinely dating, he would find a way to play with those corkscrew curls. Dinner was over before he was able to have anything close to a meaningful conversation with Araceli, but the food and music put Jade in a better mood. Perhaps she wouldn't repeat her performance.

The rainbow stretched over the city and disappeared into the mountain. As the van descended into Port au Prince, the streets grew busier and dirtier. Within six miles of the restaurant, Araceli watched another world materialize. It was like driving from the mansions of Beacon Hill to project housing Roxbury in Boston, only poorer. She thought she had been prepared growing up in a large city. She had seen US-style poverty firsthand through church service activities supervised and structured for safety and exposure. But this was beyond anything she had ever witnessed.

This was a place she could make a difference. But how to get involved? There was the Evans Foundation. But the foundation was Kyle's work, and she wasn't sure after this week she could handle being around him. It was hard enough to sit next to him in the restaurant knowing he'd kissed Jade. Or she had kissed him. Either way, Araceli couldn't risk another kiss or see him every day. Counting the driver and the guy she had kissed in a game of truth or dare when she was fourteen, she had kissed exactly three guys in her life. And every kiss had been pretend.

As soon as they reached the guesthouse, Araceli went in search of a place to be alone for a few minutes. Unfortunately, the only place affording any privacy was the bathroom. She sat on the edge of the tub and brought up the group-chat app. Hopefully someone was in a place they could answer. Her fingers flew as she typed on her phone.

So, how is your spring break? I am trying to win an Oscar on mine. Yesterday I pretended to be our Haitian driver's fiancée and even kissed him to possibly save my life. Now I need to pretend to be Kyle Evans's girlfriend because the driver's girlfriend has threatened me. I mean really threatened, as in nasty retaliation. So anyway, he kissed me. Then he kissed someone else, or she kissed him. So now I am acting like I don't care and that our kiss didn't mean anything. I know it shouldn't, but I guess having a hibernating crush on someone for fourteen years can really mess a girl up. If I can pull this off for five more days, I will be ready for a Hollywood contract. How did I get myself into this? How do I get out?

P.S. I love Haiti and working with the children. I feel like I could find purpose here if I can find a way to do it without the Evans Foundation. Mandy, do you know of any other groups?

P.P.S. He apologized for what he said when I was ten. It would be easier to fake the girlfriend thing if he hadn't. Candace, I may beat your record of most ice cream eaten in one week. Please, someone, stock up before I get back.

She stared at the screen, hoping someone would be on and respond.

Ping.

Tanner: Araceli, did you mean to send this to us?

Araceli dropped her phone on the tile floor.

Ping.
Ping.

It took her two tries to retrieve the phone. It didn't feel broken, but it was hard to see through her tears.

Ping.
Ping.

Maybe she didn't want to be able to see after all.

fifteen

JADE READ HER PHONE AND started to laugh.

Madison leaned across the board game. "Stop it, Jade. It isn't funny."

"Of course it is. Her, an actress?" Jade smirked.

The others were all reading their phones with various expressions of amusement and horror.

Kyle looked at his phone only to see the blank screen of a dead battery.

"Here." Marci thrust her phone into his hands and ran up the stairs.

Kyle read through the posts. He needed to get his group to stop talking before the guesthouse employees overheard or the other guests learned enough to gossip about it. "My group—mandatory meeting in the men's dormitory. Now."

EmilyAnne looked at him, wide-eyed.

"Only place we can all fit and shut the door. Upstairs now." Kyle herded the group into the room.

When the last person entered, Kyle closed the door. Marci and Araceli were not present. He would talk with them later as he assumed his sister had gone in search of Araceli.

Kyle held up Marci's phone. "This morning Araceli received a threatening letter. Without going into Haitian culture, let me tell you this isn't like high-school-girl kind of mean. This is ends-up-in-the-hospital mean. And if you doubt a spurned Haitian woman won't go to extremes to keep her man, ask the American owner of this guesthouse about her experiences dating her Haitian husband. I had, and do have, reason to believe Araceli could be harmed because of her pretending to be the fiancée of Aselòm to get out of the manifestation. It is imperative no one knows she is my fake girlfriend. Unfortunately, y'all found out. I ask you to please keep this quiet. Not a word about what you read tonight. Araceli's actions during the manifestation show she has a cool head. Y'all should hope you are half as inventive if you are in that situation. Any questions?" Kyle looked each participant in the eye. No one blinked. "Okay, then, I expect you will all play along and not discuss this even between yourselves. You never know who is listening or how much English they understand."

Kyle looked around the room again. He wasn't worried about the men saying something. But the women, especially Jade, might not keep their mouths shut. "For the business, we will be leaving here at 7:45 tomorrow morning and will be stopping at a place that makes cement bricks and pavers. Tanner has suggested filling the road by the culvert with them."

Kyle opened the door, and the group filed out and back downstairs.

Jade stopped and laid her hand on his arm. "I need to apologize for what I did today."

This was the last thing he wanted to deal with. "It's all good."

"Friends?"

"Just don't do anything like that again." He held out his hand and shook hers. She waited as if she wanted something more, then followed the route the others had taken downstairs.

Kyle crossed the landing to the women's dormitory and knocked on the door.

The door opened a crack, and Marci's face appeared.

"Your phone." Kyle placed it in her hand.

Marci started to close the door.

Kyle slid his foot into the crack to prevent her from shutting it. "Araceli, as soon as you are ready, please come out and talk to me. I'll be on the sofa up here on the landing."

His sister looked over her shoulder and back, giving him the tiniest of head shakes.

Kyle removed his foot and let Marci shut the door. He got his backpack and plugged in his phone. As soon as it powered up, he opened it to the chat app and reread Araceli's words.

He knew she had to be mortified, but he felt hope. Maybe there was a chance to see if there was something real between them and if they wanted it to grow.

Candace: Go talk to him!!

Tessa: Ditto, Candace.

Mandy: Don't do like I did. I regret not talking with Daniel sooner.

Zoe: But the bordello you designed . . . Oh, sorry . . . Go talk with the guy.

Abbie: I could offer to come down and take him out, but my boss has been moody lately.

Mandy: Your boss is not moody, she is expecting, but I'll pay for the ticket. But Araceli must talk with him first.

Araceli: I don't think you need to come down here and take him out. But if the offer stands for Jade . . .

I know she is going to find a way to make me even
more embarrassed over the entire thing.

Mandy: I'll send Abbie in a private jet for Jade.

Araceli smiled. She knew Mandy and Abbie weren't serious,
but it helped to know they had her back.

Candace: Are you laughing yet? Next time Jade
crosses you, think of Abbie having her pinned
against a wall, arm twisted behind her back.

Araceli: K. I'll go talk to him. The other women are
coming and getting ready for bed. Night.

Candace: Hugs from all of us. Luv you girl!

Madison knelt next to Araceli's bunk. "You okay?"

"I'll live." Araceli swung her legs over the side of the bed.
Madison pulled her into a hug and whispered, "He's sitting out
on the landing, pretending to work."

Araceli stood but looked back to make sure she hadn't left her
stomach on the bed. Madison gave her a tiny shove toward the
door. "Hurry. Jade went to the bathroom. She might not notice
you aren't here."

The first step out of the door was hardest. Kyle looked up, his
face expressionless, then smiled and scooted to the end of the
sofa, giving Araceli more than enough space to sit down.

"Thanks for coming." Kyle partially closed his laptop. "I had
a meeting and told them the truth about our relationship and
that for your safety they needed to not say anything."

Those eyes. Her resting heart rate spiked to four-hundred-
meter-dash speeds. This was such a bad idea. "Thanks." Not that it
changed what anyone had read. Heat rushed into her face. Great.
Now her cheeks matched her red-rimmed eyes.

Kyle ran his fingers along the edge of his laptop. "I know you didn't intend to text us, especially me, but I think you deserve to know my response." He opened the laptop and handed it to Araceli.

It took a moment for her to realize he had copied her conversation into a text window. Her words stared back at her with Kyle's response below them.

> My spring break? I don't get those anymore, and this trip has already been more difficult than most. Uncooperative weather and a manifestation and only 2 days in. The one bright spot is getting to know Araceli again. But despite my best efforts, I think things are turning out as poorly as when we met fourteen years ago and I called her Celi-Belly. I think she forgave me for that, but now I made a bigger mistake. She is pretending to be my girlfriend. Long story. Anyway, I kissed her, and the kiss wasn't so fake. I'm not sure where to go from here. There have been more complications, but I want to get to know the real her. Will she give me a chance?

Below the paragraph was her name with the cursor blinking after the colon. She typed back.

> Nice use of an interrobang. ?? Since it was conceptualized for rhetorical questions, I suppose you don't need an answer. Which is good, because I don't have one for you. Today has been surreal.

She handed the laptop back.

"I had no idea that mark was invented for rhetorical questions. Where do you want to go from here?" Kyle closed the laptop and set it on the side table.

Araceli resisted the urge to pull her knees up to her chin. "I know we still need to pretend to a point. And in some ways, it's easier because Madison won't ask me any questions or tease me. Jade will probably not need to play the jealous ex. But now I have embarrassed myself..."

Kyle reached for her, then stopped. "Is it terrible I am a little glad you did it? Your unwitting confession saves us both weeks of trying to figure out if the other person is interested."

Too embarrassed to answer, Araceli turned her attention to the window. What she wanted to say next had the potential to mortify her into a catatonic state, but she needed to set boundaries. She bit her lip and turned to face him. Only she couldn't look higher than the top button on his shirt. At least he'd changed out of the lipstick-stained one. "If we are going to keep faking a relationship while figuring out if there is one...That sounds weird. I have one rule. No fake kissing. If we kiss again, it can't be for any other reason than—" She looked at her hands as they twisted in her lap, then pressed them together.

Kyle briefly placed his hand on her knee and waited until she turned back to him before speaking. "I think I understand. Touch is a powerful thing. Are you all right with the hand holding and the hugs?"

"They are part of earning the Oscar." Araceli gave him her best smile.

"A daytime Emmy might be more appropriate."

"A G-rated daytime Emmy."

Kyle laughed. Even his eyes looked happy. "Agreed."

"Well, I had better go face the room now." Araceli stood to leave. Kyle stood too.

He caught her hand. "If today had turned out differently, I would give you a good night kiss." He raised her fingers to his lips and kissed them. "Good night, Celi. Don't forget the bug spray."

She pulled her hand out of his, immediately missing the contact. "Night. And thanks."

At the door, she realized she didn't really care what the other women said. She had started mending the relationship, and that was what mattered.

sixteen

ANDRÉ WAS WAITING AT THE gate when the first van pulled up. The second was still at the drainage pipe getting unloaded.

"Why isn't he in school?" asked Kyle of no one in particular.

As soon as they piled out of the van, André approached Araceli's side. "I asked everyone, and everyone says they didn't do it."

"Do what?" Araceli looked at the worried face of the director.

André beckoned, his eyes near tears as Araceli followed him into the orphanage, Kyle and the director behind them.

At the second floor, she stopped. The paint that had still been wet when she left last evening was smeared across the wall, the chalk lines she had drawn either erased or smeared beyond recognition.

She walked to the nearest wall and traced a smear with her finger. Words failed her, and she fought the urge to cry. There must be something salvageable. She was aware of voices behind her, but the words didn't register. She took a deep breath and tried to put things into perspective. Ten of the frames were smeared. That was less than 10 percent. And only three of those were badly damaged. The other seven could have a drop shadow to fix them.

Unfortunately, most of the chalk lines were obliterated, which meant two hours of work only she could do. Perhaps there was a way to speed up the process.

She felt Kyle come up behind her before he placed a protective hand on her waist. "The director says he also questioned the children. None of them claims responsibility. He feels a couple may know who did it, but their hands are clean, so to speak."

"I know it looks bad, and it's going to put me behind a few hours, but for the most part, everything is salvageable. I'm going to have to get creative in these three or four places." Araceli pointed to the areas with the most smudging. "But it isn't the end of the world. It could have been a lot worse."

Kyle leaned in close to whisper in her ear. "André feels responsible. Is there anything you can say to help him? He really does need to get to school."

Araceli nodded and turned to André. "Thank you so much for your help. I know you didn't do this. Sometimes bad things happen, and we must make the best of them. Wait until you get back from school and see what I do with this mess somebody has made." She gave him the biggest smile she could muster. André broke into a huge grin, his white teeth against his dark skin a beautiful sight.

He pointed to the worst smear. "That one is mine. I know it was meant to be little Marie's, but I traded her so she would not cry anymore."

"That is kind of you, but when I am done, she may try to get it back."

André laughed and waved as he hurried down the ramp and presumably to school.

The director spoke with Kyle in low tones. Most of the other volunteers came up the ramp. Araceli chose to ignore the shocked comments and instead walked around the walls, inspecting the damage. Who had done this wasn't nearly as important as how to fix it. She could save time by painting all the frames with help from Madison and Kate, but then the children wouldn't have the opportunity to paint their own. But she could experiment on the thirty or so frames for the infants and toddlers, plus the fifty without owners.

The storage room was exactly as she'd left it. Whoever had ruined the walls didn't have access to it. Araceli wondered who else had keys to the room besides the set she had been given. Someone came in behind her. Araceli turned to confront them.

Kyle shut the door behind him. "The director and I talked to several of the children. They still don't know who did this."

"That's what I pretty much suspected. The question being was it because of my fake engagement with Aselòm or my fake relationship with you? Either way, I have a choice. I can waste time trying to figure it out, or I can fix the mess they left me."

"I think there may be some of the original wall paint out in the storage shed."

"That might be helpful, but I'm going to see if I can paint something else over the smears." Araceli grabbed a couple of the paint cans. Without the children around for the next several hours, she should be able to work quickly. "Do you mind going and dumping out the water in the tub? And rinsing out the brushes?"

"Are you trying to get rid of me?"

"Maybe."

"You've only guaranteed I'll come back. I'll see if Marci and EmilyAnne can help you for the day. The women who are sewing don't need Marci for translation. I think they're going to be working on things for the infants and toddlers anyway."

"Thanks. Any word on whether the roof survived yesterday's rainstorm?"

Kyle hefted the tub off the shelf. "No, I'll go check as soon as I'm done rinsing these brushes."

When Araceli opened the door to let Kyle out, Madison and Kate were waiting outside.

Madison closed the door behind them. "We weren't sure if we should leave you guys alone."

Araceli shrugged. "I'm never sure either." She handed them both paint buckets. "Let's go get this fixed. I promised André he would be amazed."

"You broke the wall!" André yelled when he reached the top of the stairs.

Araceli stifled a laugh as she waited for the teen and the others to cross the room.

Sounds of disbelief echoed as the children spoke in Haitian. One of the ten-year-olds ran from the room calling, "Mr. Kyle! Mr. Kyle!"

Madison clapped her hands over her mouth to keep from laughing as the children ran their fingers over the "hole" in the wall.

"You played a joke on us. Got me good." André started laughing, and then other children joined in.

The ten-year-old returned, dragging Kyle by the hand. Ryan, Jade, Tanner, and a couple of matrons followed.

"How did you break the wall?"

Kyle's question caused André and the older children to laugh even harder. Kyle made his way through the group until he reached out and touched the cracks too.

At the confusion on his face, Araceli could no longer contain her laughter. "I didn't break the wall, I fixed it. They don't seem to make plaster-and-lath walls in Haiti."

"It looks so real."

"That's the point. I promised André I would fix this so he would be amazed."

"I am very shocked, Miss Araceli. You fooled Mr. Kyle, too." André turned to a little girl who was chattering at him like a hen scolding chicks. "Miss Marie says she wants her frame back." Disappointment showed in André's eyes, although he kept it from the rest of his features.

"Let's show her what I did with her frame first." Araceli held out a hand for the girl and guided her around the corner.

A huge smile spread over the girl's face as she reached for the flowers painted in a faux alcove next to her frame. The girl threw her arms around Araceli's waist.

Araceli smiled at André. "I think you can keep your broken wall."

André spun and hurried back around the corner, bumping Tia, who shook her finger at him. Araceli smiled at Tia following Marci's advice to let Tia speak first. A few steps brought Tia to her side inspecting the 'crack'. "Good."

"Thank you, Tia. Do you want to paint today?"

Tia shook her head and walked toward the dormitories.

Other children sought her attention, bringing Araceli's focus back to them. At least Tia spoke to her.

Kyle joined Marie in admiring the flowers. "Impressive. I thought you would need to repaint the wall and start over."

"Thank you, I had thought of repainting too. But I was able to get one of my old roommates on chat. She once painted a trompe-l'œil hallway so realistic her husband claims it gave him a concussion."

"Seriously?"

"The story is probably exaggerated, but Daniel claims running into the wall knocked enough sense into him to get him to start dating Mandy."

André returned with several children in tow. "Can we paint the rest of the frames?"

"After you have changed out of your uniforms and done whatever else you need to," Kyle answered before Araceli could.

"Then we will paint in groups of ten. André, if you could organize the groups so I have both younger and older children in each, it will be easier for everyone to help one another. Those who didn't get to finish painting their own frame can work on one for the nursery children."

André translated their directions to the other children, and within seconds the hallway was cleared of children, only the adults remaining. Marci had talked to the matrons, apparently explaining the use of the frames. Araceli wasn't sure if they were pleased or confused at the notion. Jade stood off in the corner talking with

Ryan and Tanner.

A hand on her elbow brought Araceli's attention back to Kyle. "How is André working out as a translator?"

"As you saw, he seems to be getting the message to the other children. What will he do after he ages out?"

"With his English skills, I would like to see him continue his education in the United States and then come back to help his country. I am working on a program to match sponsors and students who wish to further their education."

Marci tapped Araceli on the shoulder. "Jade claims she needs me to translate for the sewing group. Do you still need me?"

Araceli couldn't decide whether Marci was silently pleading for her to say yes.

"I could always use your help, but if Jade needs you more, I understand. Thanks for your help. I'm impressed that you guys could work from my messy sketchbooks." Araceli turned to Kyle. "Your sister could choose art school if she wants. Marci is very talented."

"No, thanks! I want to go into special education. There is such a need here. Many children don't have the chance to even learn the basics because even basic physical disabilities hamper their education. Anyway, I'll be back up if Jade doesn't really need me. EmilyAnne says she is going to keep painting." Marci headed for the closest stairway.

Kyle took Araceli's hand. "I really am impressed with what you accomplished today. You should have heard Martin telling me how you drove this huge nail in the wall and broke it to pieces. I am glad the director was still out. He might have had a heart attack."

"The look on your face when you reached the top of the ramp was priceless."

"I am finished with what I needed to do in the office today. Do you mind if I help?"

"It depends on how attached you are to this shirt." Araceli plucked at the sleeve of his white button-down.

Kyle glanced at her hand. "I have a couple T-shirts in the office I can change into. "

"Then, sure. The more, the merrier. I think we are on track to finish by Wednesday afternoon. How long is our group staying today?"

"I'd like to leave at five thirty, when the children have dinner."

"We can paint until a quarter till five. I want things to be dry when we leave."

The children started to emerge from the dormitories. Araceli found André and began giving directions.

The volunteer crew looked like they could fall asleep any moment. Boyd high-fived the men and Haitian workers. Not only had they finished sealing the roof, they'd reinstalled the solar panels before the next cloudburst. Tanner had measured both kitchens twice and was telling his plans for the remodel to anyone who would give him half an ear.

They climbed into the vans. Kyle smiled when Jade chose to take the other van with Boyd and Tanner, leaving enough room for him to slide into the middle seat next to Araceli. She tried to hide a yawn. A few dots of paint marked her face, giving her an impish air. A tired imp.

"Sorry, I didn't realize I was so tired."

"You worked hard today. I'm not sure how comfortable my shoulder is, but Marci has managed to fall asleep on it before."

Araceli poked his shoulder with her index finger. "I guess it will do."

The vans bounced along the dirt road, although they slowed down for the pipe, but this time there was no scraping sound as the van cleared the dip.

The driver cheered. "You good fix hole."

"Now if we could fill the rest of the road," said Madison as they hit a particularly deep pothole.

Marci half turned in the front seat. "I have wondered what some FDR-style projects would do for this country. Build roads, repair the wells installed after the earthquake, and fix some of the power and uneven infrastructure. Providing jobs for so many people could help."

Kyle didn't answer his sister. There was no point in debating the pros and cons of such a venture when they had no control over the outcome. Araceli leaned into his arm. Before she could entirely fall asleep, he moved his arm around her shoulder and angled his body to better cushion her.

"Thanks," she whispered without opening her eyes, her head resting above his heart. Could she hear it speed up?

The inside of the van grew silent as everyone slipped into their own thoughts or partial slumber.

Traffic was heavy but not unusual for a Monday. Moto taxis zipped between tap taps and the government cars with their flashing lights and sirens, though the latter were largely ineffectual in clearing a path. Soon the two-lane road swelled to six lanes of traffic crawling through the city. Plantain-chip sellers hawked their wares at passenger windows.

Kyle dug two dollars out of his pocket. "Marci." When she turned, he handed her the money and pointed to a seller in front of them. Marci pulled another couple bucks out of her pack, rolled down the window, and waved down a man dressed in a blue button-down and balancing a basket on his head.

"How much?" she asked in Haitian Creole.

The man responded in English. "My mother makes the best chips in all of Haiti."

"How much?" Marci repeated in English.

"For the pretty lady who ask in my language, one dollar."

Marci held up the four dollars. He gave her five bags. "Extra because you are a nice lady."

"Or because you hiked the price up," Kyle muttered.

Marci closed the window. "Of course he hiked the price up, but his mother will be happy."

"If he has one."

"Of course he does. She just might not have seen him for years." Marci smiled and handed him two bags. "Treats for the games tonight?"

"Of course."

Kyle leaned back against the headrest. How different this was than fighting the traffic on the LBJ in Dallas. It would take them as long to get to where they were going, but it felt more relaxed. Araceli sighed in her sleep. Kyle brushed a hair out of her face. He couldn't resist pulling the strand and letting it spring back. Sitting like this for another forty minutes or so was going to be a pleasure. A feeling he hadn't felt for months filled him. Contentment. It was a nice place to be.

Araceli batted at the hand trying to wake her. The dream was too lovely to give up yet.

"Celi, ma belle, wake up."

No, I'd rather stay right here with Kyle.

The hand on her shoulder shook her again. "Araceli."

She opened her eyes. Or had she? She was still very much in Kyle's arms.

He chuckled.

The pillow she had been using rumbled.

Had she drooled in her sleep? *Please, no.*

"We are almost there."

The driver honked, and the guesthouse guards rolled back the gate. Araceli sat up, the rest of the passengers were at least pretending not to pay any attention to them. Relief filled her at not seeing any moisture trailing down Kyle's shirt.

He rubbed her cheek with his thumb. "You picked up a crease line from my shirt.

She raised her hand, trapping his. Someone opened the van door. It may have been the light, but for a moment she could have sworn she saw something like desire in his eyes before he pulled his hand away, bringing hers with it.

Kyle adjusted his hand, linking it with hers. "Come on."

If only reality would end the same way her dream almost had.

seventeen

KYLE STEPPED OUT OF THE shower, his flip-flops squeaking against the tile floor. He dried himself off and reapplied mosquito repellent. One of the few things he didn't enjoy about Haiti was the constant need to wear the odious cologne, but the little pests had a peculiar affinity for him. One had managed to bite him on the palm of his hand last visit. Unlike many of the volunteers, he chose not to wear shorts most of the trip, as his pretreated pants offered him better protection.

The guesthouse did a great job of keeping the mosquitoes out, but a few unguarded seconds was all it took to be bitten. But that was not the itch bothering him now. Ever since Araceli had fallen asleep in his arms last evening on the drive back from the orphanage, he wanted to spend more time with her. Last night they'd ended up on separate teams for Pictionary, a game she should be banned from on principle. He hadn't managed another moment alone with her all evening.

One of his old T-shirts would do for today. If Tanner didn't need him on the remodel, he could go paint. He needed to go to the building supply with the men this morning to purchase fixtures, so he wouldn't get to ride in the same van as Araceli, but if he were lucky, he might catch a moment or two with her before breakfast.

"Hey, guys, the vans will be here in an hour." He knocked on the ends of the bunks as he made his way to the door. He could hear his sister and several of the other women in the dining room below. Their voices crescendoed as he descended the stairs.

"Here is Kyle. He can decide." Jade raised her fork in his direction. "We were discussing an alternative to going to Jacmel on Thursday."

Kyle picked up a plate and looked over the buffet. "As I explained, I need to go to Jacmel on an assignment. So we are taking all of you to the southern coast."

"Why do we have to go with you? Why can't one van go north to Labadee and the other down to Jacmel? Marci can go with us, and you can still go south."

After adding one more piece of mango to his plate, Kyle sat next to his sister, as Araceli was sandwiched between Madison and Kate. "What do you think of this plan?" he asked his sister.

"I don't care much, but I would like to show EmilyAnne Labadee. After experiencing the real Haiti, seeing the tourist version almost makes you wonder if you are in the same country. We hardly need an interpreter to go to cruise-ship town anyway."

"Last night Tanner asked me about skipping the Jacmel excursion as he wants the time to work on the kitchen. Since the director will be around, I was going to make sure he could be available to supervise and interpret if necessary. So maybe we need to have a discussion once the rest of them get down here."

Jade smiled triumphantly.

Kyle suppressed a sigh. More than likely, Jade would get her way. He turned his attention to Araceli and was rewarded with a smile.

"It's a trap," mouthed Araceli before taking a sip of her water.

"I know," he mouthed back. It was nice to have an ally.

"All last night we listened to Jade outline the wonders of Labadee." Madison used her fingers to number the points.

"Swimming in the ocean, shopping, dining, the scenery, and a chance to relax. What do you have to say to entice us to go to Jacmel? Marci didn't seem to know, other than what you had already told us about going to some school."

Kyle set down his fork. "There is ocean down there too. The school is a project one of the board members has taken on. This particular board member has a huge heart but a limited pocketbook. She helped the mothers fill out an application for one of the foundation's grants. We were somewhat surprised at how little they asked for. The school is largely funded by the mothers' own efforts. They sell various handicrafts and do odd jobs to keep the school running. They added a small flock of chickens and are looking to expand their fold so they can not only use the eggs to feed the school children but sell them to help cover the cost of the teacher. I want to visit to determine what needs we can help with without undermining the efforts of the mothers. I was supposed to visit last month, but some other things came up. I can't skip this."

"Is this one of those delicate-line issues you were discussing between giving a hand up and a handout?" asked Chelsea.

"I think so. The mothers are going to a lot of work to keep their children in school. We want to help them to do that, as the alternative is—" To be blunt or not? Kyle always struggled with this part of the conversation. "Children who are not educated end up working. Many times, they end up being a restavek—a type of houseslave that is almost always over worked, underfed, and often abused. The mother may believe she has found a job for her son or daughter, or she may even know to some extent as she may have been a restavek herself. It is estimated more than one in fifteen Haitian children live in slavery."

Araceli set her spoon down. "How can the mothers let that happen?"

"When it comes down to a choice between putting food in your children's mouths and sending an older child off to live with an 'uncle' to work and be fed, desperation takes over. I imagine they try not to think too hard about what could happen."

Marci joined the conversation. "The sad thing is so many mothers believe the lie that their children are better off in an orphanage than with them. The cycle perpetuates itself. And you end up with three and four generations of children being raised by orphanages. And no matter how hard we try, in the end an employee's love will never be the same as a mother's."

All the men had arrived during the conversation. The women remained around the table. "As soon as y'all get your food, we will have a short meeting," Kyle instructed them all.

Most of the women cleared their dishes while they waited.

"A proposal has been made that on Thursday we divide into two groups so y'all can visit the resort town of Labadee. Tanner asked last night if he could continue to work on the kitchens as he is afraid that taking a day off will put him behind. I told him I would talk with the director today. I still need to go to Jacmel. So, I would like to know what y'all want to do."

Brandon raised his hand. "If Tanner needs help, I would rather help him."

"I already told Tanner I'd work with him," said Boyd.

"I'll second that. Although it would be nice to do some sightseeing, I want to leave on Saturday knowing everything is finished," said Ryan.

"So, we have six seats in the van. Though it's likely they won't, Marci needs to go with the resort group in case they need an interpreter. EmilyAnne, would you rather go with Marci?"

EmilyAnne gave an affirmative nod.

"That leaves four seats. Who wants to go north?"

Jade, Chelsea, and Kate raised their hands immediately.

"Madison and Araceli, do you want to go to Jacmel, then?"

Madison answered first. "I am torn. I want to go to both."

"I have been looking forward to seeing how the school runs. Your mother mentioned it when we talked." Araceli gave a little smile.

Kyle thought Madison had poked Araceli under the table. "I'll talk with the drivers and the director today and let you know tonight if the plan is going to work." He looked at his watch. "The vans should be here in fifteen minutes. My van will be going to the lumber supply, Marci's straight to the orphanage. Araceli, do you need any more supplies?"

"I could use some sponge brushes."

"Then come with us. Anything else?"

There were a few head shakes.

"Okay, fifteen minutes."

Kyle grabbed a bottle of water to brush his teeth before following the others upstairs. He couldn't recall looking forward to the lumber store quite so much. Even with the guys, he would get a bit of time with Araceli.

The handprint animals had looked easier to create on Pinterest. Even with Marci and Kyle explaining to the workers and children and with the pictures she'd printed, the elephant and the giraffe resembled aardvarks more than they did their own species. If it wasn't for the giggles of the children as they finger painted spots on lions and stripes on bears, Araceli might have given up in frustration. The morning was carefully coordinated so that after each child finished their animal, they were whisked away for their bath. The baby gates at the end of the hallway kept freshly bathed children from returning for another round.

"I think Darwin missed this one." Kyle pointed to an animal that may have been an octopus more than any mammal known to roam the seven continents.

Marci painted an eye on the animal. "You mean the octopotomus? Really, brother, you need to watch more *Animal Planet*. Last week they featured it after the elusive spotted ape."

"Don't forget the pandaroo," called Madison.

"Or the zebrino." Kate pressed a child's hand to the wall and received a squeal of laughter as thanks.

Hands on her hips, the head nursery matron spoke with Kyle. Araceli watched as his words defused the woman's anger.

After she left, Kyle turned to the group. "She says no more. The paint is too hard to get off, and the children are trying to paint the other walls with water."

"Oops. I didn't see that one coming. But then, I tested the idea with my nephew over Skype." Araceli cleaned her hand with a baby wipe.

Madison looked up from where she was adding eyes to her animal. "We could finish them ourselves. We might even get an elephant with a trunk."

"I was going to let the older children help, but if it is hard to clean off…"

Kyle stretched as he stood. Araceli's heart gave an extra couple of beats of appreciation for the muscle tone the old T-shirt showed off. "Have you promised the older children they could make animals, or even mentioned it?"

It took a moment for Araceli's distracted brain to process the words. "I don't think so. I told André I was going to work on the animals with the toddlers, so he didn't worry about us finishing the frames without them."

"Good enough. If you didn't make any promises, we don't need to wait to finish these."

They worked for the next hour. The hand animals went ever so much faster not having to keep wiggly children still.

Chelsea began to laugh. "Oh no. Look at the creature between my giraffe and the monkey. It looks like they had a baby."

Araceli looked up from her pink flamingos and laughed. "Darwin missed another one."

Madison walked over from where she was working. "I wonder how long it will take before the teens use whatever biology they have learned to make the connection."

Kyle stood. "If they are looking at mine, they will assume it was from an alien invasion."

Everyone laughed.

A matron stuck her head into the hall and shushed them.

Araceli checked the time on her phone. "We need to do a few more palm trees and bushes. Then we'll be done. I'd like this hallway to be dry by the time the others get back from school."

Fifteen minutes later they started their cleanup. Kyle handed Araceli a baby wipe. "Either you are growing a lion mane, or Midas touched your cheek."

Araceli raised the wipe to her cheek.

"Other side." Kyle pointed to a spot below his own cheekbone.

Araceli tried to find the same place on her face.

Kyle covered her hand with his and gently rubbed, then took a step closer and raised her chin. "You have some more here."

Araceli dropped her hand, nearly placing it on his chest before thinking better of it. His shirt still looked clean. She looked back to his face as he moved to another spot. She hadn't noticed the fine lines at the corners of his eyes before. Smile—not squint—lines. Kyle stopped rubbing and for a long moment just looked at her.

A million tiny questions rushed through Araceli's mind, but before any of them formed a complete thought, Madison cleared her throat and Kyle stepped back.

He handed the wipe back. "I think I got it all." He stepped over the child gate and walked to his office.

Araceli turned to Madison, hoping Madison would speak first because she doubted her voice would sound normal.

Madison obliged. "I was going to ask where you wanted the paint, but maybe I should ask if you'd rather I didn't go to Jacmel."

"Let's put the paint in the upstairs classroom." Araceli grabbed a can. She didn't have an answer to the other question. If Madison didn't go to Jacmel, she would have a day alone with Kyle and the driver. Was her heart racing out of fear or anticipation? Araceli wasn't sure.

A commotion from the front of the building drew Kyle from his office.

"This is not the plywood we chose." Tanner told the driver.

Aselòm looked at Kyle when he answered. "It was what was on the dock when I went back to pick it up. It looked the same to me."

Kyle stepped between Tanner and the driver. The problem more than likely was the result of a switch made by the store. "Did you inspect every piece when you bought it or just the first few on the top of the pile?"

"I looked at the first three and then told the worker I would take fifteen pieces."

"Is it all marked the same?" Kyle had learned a bit over the years and knew the plywood should be stamped with the grade.

Boyd, Tanner, and Brandon lifted each piece and checked it. "It is all marked the same, but some of it is not the same quality."

"We have a couple choices. We can take it back and spend a half day fighting the store, or figure out how to make do with the wood we have. Sadly, it is all marked the same grade, so it is going to be hard to trade."

Wordlessly, Tanner pulled a tape measure from his pocket and made several measurements. "It is the center of the wood with the problem. I think we can cut out the cabinets and avoid the centers, but I may need one or two more sheets, and I am already at budget."

"I'll make up the budget loss. It is better than losing time." Boyd reached for his wallet.

Kyle stopped him. "No need. I plan on a reserve budget whenever we have a building project since we always seem to need it. The variable quality of goods here is why I asked you to buy the hinges in the United States."

"Let's get this lumber to the back porch. We have cabinets to build."

Kyle turned to Aselòm and reassured him in Haitian, "This wasn't your fault. I told the guy at the store to hand select every piece of wood we bought, but I was busy elsewhere and didn't remind him again."

"No problem, boss. You were with Miss Araceli. I see why you want to be with her instead of men. She is beautiful and patient with all the children. She best woman you ever bring here. Will you bring her back?"

"If she is willing to come again."

"My girlfriend is not angry at her anymore and finally believes I not cheating on her. I wish I knew she was your woman or I—"

Kyle placed a hand on Aselòm's shoulder. "Don't worry. You got her out of the manifestation safely. Nothing else matters. Now, I need to talk with you and the other drivers about Thursday. Let's go find them."

The last of the children were painting the final touches on their frames. Tia added flowers to hers following the technic of dipping her brush in multiple colors Araceli demonstrated. Getting to know the girl with the soulful eyes was not as easy as Araceli anticipated. Spending any one-on-one time with the older children was difficult as they grouped around her, each wanting attention. She didn't have enough arms for the hugs or hours to talk with them all.

André walked around and talked to each one encouragingly. Araceli worked on adding a few more trompe-l'œil details to the wall so the flowers and crumbled wall were not the only points of interest.

Chelsea came upstairs with Jade. "We need to get some photos."

Araceli watched as they gathered the children in groups and posed in front of the wall. Jade handed out clean brushes and told two or three children to pretend they were still painting. For a couple of the photos, Jade even ordered the volunteers to pick up a brush. Occasionally Marci would take a child out of the grouping. Oddly, Jade didn't protest her choreographed masterpiece getting unbalanced.

"I think we have enough now." Chelsea put her camera away.

Marci led the group of children she'd pulled out of the other photos over to Chelsea. "You need to take a couple photos of them."

"I thought you said they couldn't be photographed."

"Their photos can't be used outside of approved board uses, but they need to have their picture taken just as much." Marci left them and came to stand by Araceli as Jade choreographed several shots.

Araceli dipped her brush in a deep blue. "Why did you do that?"

"Some children can't have their photos on the website or social media. Some of them are in the adoption process. Others for their own protection."

"So, am I done here? I need to take some photos of the men building the cabinets," said Chelsea.

"Did you get any photos with Araceli?" asked Marci.

Chelsea aimed her camera at Marci and Araceli and took a couple of photos.

Marci jumped out of the way. "Not with me in them. André come over here, and Marie and Tia and you two." She pointed to a couple more children. Araceli put her arm around Tia's shoulders. Tia leaned into the half-hug.

Jade didn't orchestrate the photo, and Araceli sighed in relief when Chelsea finished taking a couple shots and left. Posing for pictures wasn't her favorite thing. It must not be Marci's either. She'd managed to duck almost every photo taken on the trip so far. Araceli needed to take lessons.

Kyle came up the ramp. "It's four thirty. Do you need help cleaning up?"

"I'm going to finish up with this hibiscus before I clean up." Araceli looked around the room. "But it looks like there is plenty to clean."

"You have red paint on your forehead." Kyle handed her the baby wipe container.

"And you didn't even get a spot of paint on your shirt. How do you do it?" Araceli wiped a baby wipe across her face. Yup, red paint. It would have been in the photo too.

Kyle made a show of checking his T-shirt. "I guess I am naturally clean."

Araceli raised her brush full of hibiscus-red paint. "I could change that for you." She aimed the brush for his nose.

He caught her wrist only inches from his face. "Don't start something you don't want the children to imitate."

"Sorry, I wasn't thinking." She dropped her brush back to her palette.

Kyle leaned close enough to whisper in her ear. "If they were not around, I would have let you and got you back. I like flirting with you, Celi, ma belle."

Araceli nearly dropped her palette. She could feel her face heating to the shade of red on her paintbrush. The turn of the old phrase calling her his beautiful Celi robbed her of any other thought. "I … um, you could start cleaning in the classroom."

Kyle took a step away, then back toward her. "Madison told me she wants to go to Labadee, so that means it would just be the two of us for Jacmel. You okay without a crowd?"

Yes! No! Maybe? "It's fine."

"I'll arrange for the SUV, then." Kyle smiled at her before he walked away.

Her hand was shaking as she lifted the brush to the flower.

The news that there would be an excursion to Labadee was well received. The director arranged to stay at the orphanage all day Thursday on the condition that Aselòm remain with the men since they might need a driver. Kyle considered this more than fair as Aselòm spoke the best English and often stayed around during the day to help with the construction. This meant Kyle needed to send his second-favorite driver with the trip north. It left Kyle with Kervens.

Kervens only spoke common English phrases. Not only would Kyle be basically alone with Araceli all day, the driver wouldn't be able to understand most of what they talked about. Considering he'd come close to kissing Araceli twice today, the relative privacy might not be a good thing.

Kyle ran his hand through his hair. He wasn't here to flirt. But it was the Caribbean—it was supposed to be romantic.

Double-checking his mosquito netting, he laid his head on the pillow. He wondered if Araceli was having as hard a time falling asleep as he was.

eighteen

PARASITES. ARACELI TRIED NOT TO think of the word as she rinsed her hair. The reason they were told to wear flip-flops in the shower was parasites. Brushing their teeth with bottled water because the tap water wasn't safe to drink hadn't been hard to get used to, but as she wrung the water out of her hair, she couldn't help but wonder what might still be lurking in it. She blamed her jitters on Kate, who'd emerged from her shower last night in a state of near panic after seeing a bug in the bathroom. Parasites were too small to be seen.

Between nightmares of giant bugs growing out of everyone's head and feet, and dreams of Kyle, she had a restless night. The worst was when a parasite growing out of Kyle's head wanted to kiss her.

Araceli dried her hair the best she could. She would need to put it up before they left for the orphanage in an hour. If only she'd thought to bring a blow dryer, but she hadn't known if it would survive the electricity issues. The guesthouse boasted excellent wiring—at least Kyle trusted the power enough to plug in his computer.

Last night, before Kate had lost it over the showers, Jade had said some seemingly inappropriate things to Marci about the family's wealth. Araceli didn't think of the Evans family in terms of dollars. She had been in her late teens before she'd realized they were anything other than middle class. Mr. Evans was just one of Dad's friends. Jade's family, by all accounts, was also wealthy, so it struck Araceli as odd she would be so concerned about Kyle's net worth.

Someone tapped on the bathroom door.

"In a minute!" Araceli threw on an old T-shirt bearing the paint of several different projects. She should have taken Candace's advice and brought a couple of nicer shirts. But she wasn't trying to impress her fake boyfriend anyway.

She could have sworn the face in the mirror called her a liar.

Not wishing to stay in the room and hear more gossip, Araceli slipped out to the terrace. It was warm enough out there that maybe her hair could dry faster.

She found a spot with no shadows, leaned over, and ran her fingers through her hair, trying to separate the strands. Then she whipped her head back and forth, forcing the air through the strands until she was nearly dizzy.

"Is that as fun as it looks?"

Araceli straightened so fast she nearly lost her balance, but Kyle grabbed her arm, saving her from further embarrassment. "Careful there."

Araceli lifted the hair out of her face. "Morning. You should try it. Twice as fun as a blow dryer." He didn't have any parasites sticking out of his head. But did he have to look so put together in his shirt and khakis? *GQ* cover model versus too pathetic for secondhand. Jade was right about one thing. Kyle was definitely out of her league. Now, if her heart would listen to her mind and slow down. Not happening.

He reached for a strand and wound it around his finger. "This is the first time I have seen you with your hair down."

"After reading about scabies and lice, I figured I best keep my hair up. These silly curls attract the darnedest things."

"Like men?"

"No! Like flying bugs and stuff." Stupid blush. She didn't need a mirror to know her face had turned a deep pink.

Kyle stepped into her space. "They probably attract more men than you know."

"You saw the chat the other night, so you know that isn't true." Her cheeks were burning. No wonder they called it fire-engine red.

"Being attracted by beauty is easy. The bravery needed to act on the attraction is hard." He tucked the lock he was toying with behind her ear. "Ready for breakfast?" He offered his arm. Araceli took it. She could get used to dating someone who treated her like this.

So far, the day was running smoothly. The on-site nurse had completed the immunizations for several of the infants and toddlers. Kyle was no stranger to the controversies on social media about vaccines, but they'd never witnessed what disease could do in a third-world country. The nurse helped him bring the records up-to-date. Marci entered the new files into his laptop. One of his pet projects was to get all the orphanage records digitized. They would still need a paper copy on the premises as even dial-up would be iffy if the electricity weren't an issue. But the electronic records would be a backup if the paper ones were destroyed.

"The *K*'s are done. Will you hand me the *L*'s?" Marci's request interrupted his thoughts. Just as well, as they would have ended up on Araceli in a moment. Kyle set the folders for the *L* section on the desk near Marci.

Marci didn't open the folders. "So, I am curious. You told everyone on Monday night you were faking the entire dating thing, but I saw you clean paint off Araceli's face in the nursery hall yesterday. You can't act *that* well. What's up with you and Araceli?"

Kyle pulled up a plastic chair. "I'd say none of your business, but I think you are right, or at least I hope you are."

"To be clear—this isn't fake?"

"Wipe that silly smile off your face. I don't know how to fake what I am feeling."

"I knew it! That is why I suggested to Jade that two groups wouldn't be a problem. Tanner already asked me about not going, and I told him to talk to you."

"Are you trying to play matchmaker?"

"Not at first, but the more I watch her ... she doesn't seem to be whiny or anything. And she isn't after your money. After Jade's comments last night, I think I'd know that." Marci opened the top file.

"What did Jade say last night?"

"Same old stuff. Prying about how the fortune will be divided, how many cousins I have, etc. The conversation started with me reminding her I didn't want my photo all over social media showing I was in Haiti. Then she went on this rant about how dumb it was I went to public school, even a magnet school."

"Some days I wonder how Cassie and Jade became friends. Sometimes I think Mom wants me to give her a second chance."

"I think Mom just wants you to get settled. Maybe because Grandpa is getting older and stuff. Anyway, Jade survived Haiti, which is on your list. But as far as that item, Araceli seems to be thriving here. She even asked André to teach her a few Haitian words."

"I didn't know that." Kyle refiled the *K* folders in the cabinet.

"I bet you could teach her some Haitian tomorrow. *Mwen renmen w.*"

I love you? "I'm not ready to say that."

Ban m yon ti bo."

Kyle walked behind Marci's chair and kissed the crown of her head.

She batted him away. "That is not what I meant."

"But you said 'Give me a kiss.'"

Marci blew out an exasperated puff of air. "I was thinking of Haitian-Creole words you could teach Araceli."

"Any more advice?"

"Whatever you do, eat lunch someplace reputable so you don't get food poisoning."

"I'll do that. I'm going to go check on the group projects. Do you need anything?"

"Bring me back a water, please."

Kyle saluted and left the office, heading for the kitchen first to see Tanner's progress. He would check on the painting last.

At least Marci hadn't mentioned *"Eske ou ta vle marye avèk mwen?"* because for the first time in a long time, *the* question had crossed his mind. But it was far too soon to talk marriage.

"Ladies, we did it. I am declaring the painting phase complete." Araceli cleaned off her brush.

"Are you sure? There are still yards and yards of walls."

"Careful—I still have some paint, and there are no children around to witness." Araceli air painted a mustache on Madison.

Kate dropped her paintbrush in the water basin. "It looks amazing. I'll admit I thought Jade was right when she told you the mural was a dumb idea last February. I am glad I got assigned to your team."

"I'm glad you two were on my team too. I can't wait to get the clipboards up and see the kids display their first art pieces."

Madison used a hammer to replace the lid on a can of green paint. "How are you going to put the boards on the cement wall?"

"I have a glue for cement. My roommates and I tested five different kinds on the walls of the tornado shelter of the house I live in. Not sure how we will use the clipboards in the shelter. We haven't used the room since my sophomore year."

"You get tornadoes up in Indiana?" asked Kate.

"Not as often as Oklahoma or Texas, but one came through about four years ago and ripped out several houses. Fortunately there were no deaths. We have had minor ones since then." Araceli pulled the painter's tape from the walls.

Kate joined her in removing the tape. "How long does the glue take to dry?"

"It takes twelve hours to be completely solid, but after a minute of holding the board in place, it usually stays. The big problem will be keeping the kids from playing with them today. Although they do seem to listen to André's directions."

Madison put her hands on her hips. "I think your biggest problem won't be the children. It will be whoever vandalized the project last time."

Once they finished cleaning up, Araceli got the glue and caulk guns from storage. Madison and Kate matched the decorated clipboards with the frames on the wall. They set up an assembly line of sorts, taking turns applying the glue to the wall and then holding each clipboard in place for sixty seconds. They were only a third of the way through when the unmistakable cacophony of seventy children returning from school filled the building.

Araceli bit her lip. Could the children help with this part? André came up the ramp with several children. Araceli hurried to intercept them.

"It is imperative you don't touch the clipboards on the walls until tomorrow after school. The glue needs to dry."

André translated.

The children nodded their understanding.

"I could use some strong and patient helpers. Once the glue is on the clipboards, the boards must be held in place for one full minute." Araceli pointed to Madison, who was in the process of doing what she described. "Sixty seconds seems like ten minutes when holding the boards in place, so you must be very patient. Also, you must tell me if any glue gets on you as soon as possible."

André translated, and five boys raised their hands. "Miss Araceli, these boys want to help. Most of the girls want to go sew since it's the last day before they get to have a fashion show. And I told the younger ones this job was not for them."

"Thanks, André. Go change out of your uniforms, boys, and I'll see you back in a minute. Remember, please, please don't touch the boards on the wall."

Tia raised her hand. "I will make signs in English, French, and Haitian. 'Danger: No Touching.' Will that help?"

"Great idea! Merci." Araceli gave the girl a smile. They'd had a few short conversations over the last few days, but this was the first time she had volunteered.

With the help of the boys and another caulk gun and glue, they were able to get through more boards.

Kate took out her bandanna and wiped her face. "I feel like I am melting today."

Araceli reached for her water bottle. "I miss the breeze that has been here each afternoon. André, where did it go?"

The boy shrugged. "You are not used to Haiti. This is not even hot."

"I grew up in Texas, but heat is different here without air-conditioning." Kate fanned herself with a clipboard.

"I'm sure we can survive. Back to work, ladies." Araceli aimed her caulk gun at the wall and applied glue to the next square.

Some of the children who had been watching left the room. They returned a few minutes later with two battery-powered floor fans.

"My heroes!" Madison clapped her hands.

Araceli thanked each of them, glad the French and Haitian words for *thank you* sounded nearly identical.

Kyle came up the stairs, then walked over to a clipboard and raised a hand to touch it. Several children yelled, "No, Mr. Kyle!" in unison, then explained in all three languages how he couldn't touch the boards. He held up his hands in surrender and reassured them he understood before coming to where Araceli stood. "I understand a fate worse than missing ten dinners awaits me if I touch a board."

"I made no such threat, but I am happy to know they took me seriously."

"Do you need any help?"

"Sure. I hope you are a patient man. Holding these boards in place for an entire minute is not as easy as it sounds."

André shook out his hands. "She is telling the truth. I thought it was another joke when she said it was a hard job."

Araceli gave him a smile. "And you are all doing an excellent job. And the fans the others brought in is making it easier."

"*Pouvons-nous chanter?*" asked one of the boys.

"Of course you may sing. It will help the time pass more quickly. And I would like to learn some of your songs," Araceli answered back in French. Far more of the children understood the language, as it was required in school.

"Be careful which songs you choose. Not all of the songs you know are appropriate for a nice lady like Miss Araceli to learn." Kyle looked at each boy in turn.

"No worries, Mr. Kyle. We only teach her the nice songs."

By the time they finished, Araceli had learned several songs. And taught them a French song a few of the children had heard before.

As she put away the glue and caulk guns, Araceli hummed one of the tunes. She was tired, sweaty, and happy. She jumped when the storeroom door shut behind her.

Kyle handed her a roll of tape. "Don't lose this."

She took the other side of the spool, but Kyle didn't release his side. Instead, he used it to pull her toward him.

"What are you doing?"

"I haven't had a chance to talk to you since this morning."

"We were talking out there."

"That isn't what I mean. And besides, we haven't been doing spectacularly at our fake-dating thing. And I figured a minute or two in the storage closet would give them something to wonder about." He released his side of the tape.

Araceli rolled her eyes. "You are incorrigible."

"And you are adorable when you are happy. But I would be careful about humming that song. It is about a mermaid luring a man away. If you sing the tune to me, I might follow you to the depths of the sea."

"I thought the song was about a whale."

"The whale saves the man. Even if he doesn't want to be saved." Kyle kissed her cheek and left the room.

Araceli stood frozen. What was she supposed to think?

nineteen

Roosters crowed, and the eastern sky lightened enough to outline the trees. Kyle handed Araceli a granola bar, a mango, and a water bottle. They met the driver at the gate. The group going to Labadee wouldn't be leaving for another hour. Neither would the men working on the kitchen repairs.

By avoiding early morning traffic, Kyle hoped to shorten the four-hour trip to Marigot, which was less than one hundred kilometers away. Seven hours in a car with Araceli. Now, if he could start a conversation.

They drove through the city. Businesses had not yet opened, leaving the road open for delivery trucks and various embassy vehicles. Only a handful of tap taps ran. Bags of garbage awaited pickup next to the ever-present cinder-block walls.

Araceli broke the silence. "Why Haiti? I mean, of all the charitable work your family does or could do, you spend so much time here and keep your spending, which could be considerable, to a minimum to help just one place."

"Other charities work in Haiti with a broader spectrum and even more money, but Haiti is personal to my mother. Before she inherited Grandma's position as head of the family charities, her heart was in Haiti because of a pen pal she wrote in the seventh grade. Once she convinced Dad to marry her—a long story—she insisted they honeymoon in Haiti. At the time, Baby Doc was still in power, so the situation was worse than what it is today. Anyway, Mom couldn't find her friend. But what she did find…well, you can guess. She took part of her inheritance and founded the Evans Foundation, separate from Grandfather's charities. She started by just making donations but learned the money rarely made it to the orphans. So she initiated a more hands-on approach. Since the foundation doesn't bear my grandfather's name, most people don't make the connection. We try to keep it that way and maintain a low profile when we are down here. Having a different last name helps. People at the embassy want us to have bodyguards when we are here, but that would make us stand out. As it is, very few people know where we are on the *Forbes* lists."

"Is that why Marci didn't want Jade and Chelsea to take her photo?"

"Pretty much. With social media, our lives are not as private as we would like. Marci chose to go to a public high school, so she tries to stay out of the spotlight."

"I understand your mother's passion for the country. After this week, I want to do more, though I don't know how. For a while now I have felt like I chose a worthless major. In a month and a half, I graduate, and then what? It isn't like painting helps people."

Kyle reached for Araceli's hand and ran his thumb over her knuckles while he thought of an answer. The first one through his mind didn't sound rational. If Araceli was by his side, they could do so much together. "Did you see those children's faces this week? Art made a difference for them. Not only that, but children who have gone through trauma can often express themselves in art. Have you heard of art therapy?"

"My old roommate Mandy suggested it, but I'd need to take so many classes before I could even start grad school, and I am not sure I am ready to commit three more years of my life to school.

Writing has never been my forte, and frankly, it scares me." The last part came out in a whisper as she turned to the window.

Kyle continued to run his thumb over her knuckles. "Maybe there are other paths to your goal. I don't think the children care about a degree." He turned her hand over and started tracing her palm.

As he hoped, Araceli turned back toward him. "Do you have any ideas?"

"Maybe. I'll let you know if I have anything concrete. So, what drew you to art?"

The next couple of hours flew by as they talked about subjects ranging from art to childhood pranks to favorite bands. It was the most pleasant drive Kyle had ever taken.

The school was not what Araceli expected. The walls reminded her of industrial wood pallets. Trees on the far side of the school were visible through the three-inch gaps between the slats. Araceli followed Kyle to the open doorway. Children dressed in mis-matched red-and-blue uniforms sat on rough wooden benches. A teacher stood in front of a weathered blackboard teaching a lesson in French. She knew from their earlier conversation that the teacher made eighty dollars a month—a sum the mothers of the children sacrificed and scrimped to pay. Before they could create too much of a distraction, they stepped back.

Kyle motioned for her to follow him over to a chicken coop that looked better constructed than the school.

Kyle shook his head. "The school turned in a grant request for more chickens."

"Surely they need more money."

"I see why our board member fell in love with this school and the mothers who are so dedicated to keeping it open." A few women gathered at the edge of the schoolyard. Kyle took Araceli's hand and walked over to them.

He started the introductions in Haitian, but one of the women interrupted him in English.

"You speak good Creole, but they asked me to translate."

"What if I speak in Creole, and if I get something wrong you can correct me?"

The women conversed, and Kyle joined in. Araceli tried to follow the conversation, but so few of the words mirrored French it was impossible to make heads or tails of what they were saying. She chose to study the children while she waited. Did they understand the difference education could make in their lives? Or did they view school as something they had to endure? Araceli was still contemplating the matter when Kyle joined her.

"Spying on them?"

"Observing."

"The children will have a break in a few minutes, then we can meet them. I brought some pencils to hand out and some extra eggs from the hunt, with stickers. Can you help me put the two together quickly?"

Araceli followed Kyle to the car, where he pulled out a duffel and set it on the hood.

"There are twenty-three children. I think I have about fifty eggs."

They quickly filled the eggs with stickers and some hard candies. The pencils came in a conglomeration of colors, the type purchased for school or birthday parties. She finished folding the ends of the last cardboard egg as the children exited the schoolhouse.

As Kyle spoke with them, Araceli made a vow to learn Haitian so she could understand what the big smiles meant. Kyle pointed to her, and the children clapped.

The mother who'd translated before leaned over. "Your husband says you will give each child two eggs and that he is giving us fifteen chickens now and fifteen in the fall."

Araceli turned to correct the woman but noticing the tears in her eyes decided to let the misconception go. The children gathered around as Araceli handed out the eggs while Kyle let each one choose two pencils from his stash. Several of the children hugged her around the waist. Each told her *mèsi*, which, being so close to *merci*, was easy enough to understand.

All too soon they were saying their good-byes and getting back in the car.

"I've never seen a woman cry over chickens before," said Araceli.

"I wanted to give them ten times what they asked for when we drove up and I saw the condition of their school. All they asked for was money for more chickens. They could have asked for so much more. I also told them I would like to pay for the teachers for this month and next. It is an interesting balance. These women have learned to fish, so to speak, but they need a stocked pond."

She pondered the analogy. "Makes sense. I wish I understood more Creole. I want to speak with the children."

"That I can help with." Kyle pointed out his window. *"Lanmè:* ocean."

Araceli repeated the word, and they played the game all the way to Jacmel, where they stopped for lunch. Before going into the restaurant, they stopped at a little store. Kyle picked up a couple of chocolate bars. "Askanya chocolate. From bean to bar, the entire process happens here."

"You sound like a commercial."

"Wait until you taste it."

Araceli reached for a bar, but Kyle kept them out of reach. "After lunch." They entered a tiny restaurant.

When Kyle finished the last bite on his plate, he asked, "Did you wear your swimsuit?"

"Yes, are you finally going to tell me why? *Lanmè?"*

"No, someplace far better. We will need to walk, but it is worth every step."

"I'm fine with hiking." She held out her hand. "Chocolate?"

Kyle gave her a bar and took her hand and led her out of the restaurant. "Then let's see if Kervens found any new shortcuts."

The dirt parking lot marked the head of the trail—and was as far as the four-wheel-drive SUV could take them, having already crossed the Jacmel river and several kilometers of unpaved roads. A guide waited to help them along the trail for one hundred gourde each.

"I thought you said this was a difficult hike." Araceli walked beside him.

"Don't be deceived. But like most difficult things, it will be worth it." The trail was uncrowded, giving Kyle hope they would have the same once they reached the pools. Soon the climb became steeper and more treacherous, the guide helping them over a couple sections.

Araceli took Kyle's hand to steady herself as she scrambled over a rock. "I believe you now."

They came to the first of the three basin ponds. Last time he'd visited here, the rains had turned the pools murky. Today they were clear.

"What is this place?"

"Bassin Cheval, actually the first of three pools and waterfalls making up Bassin Bleu. This one is the shallowest. I hope you are not afraid of swimming or doing a bit of rappelling." Kyle held out his hand to steady Araceli as she descended a particularly steep spot. He bit his tongue about what lay ahead of them.

"That is an interesting combination." She gave him a skeptical look.

They hiked around to the second pool, Bassin Palmiste. Only three other people were there with a guide in one of the picnic areas. They stopped to take a photo.

Their guide helped them over a stream and around the bend to the last pool. Araceli gasped. "This blue is amazing. It's turquoise—no, it's … I am not sure I have the proper word in my color vocabulary."

"Bassin Clair or Bleu, depending on who you ask."

"Such an unimaginative name."

"This is where we take off our shoes and extra clothes. Kervens will take our bags back to the last pool."

"How will we get back?" She pulled off her shirt. The modest navy one-piece suit she wore underneath fit her personality. She blushed and turned away when she caught him looking.

Kyle pointed to the end of the pool. "The same way the water does, more or less."

The guide readied the rope to help them rappel down a flight of worn steps carved into the stone to the pool. They walked a couple more yards to a spot four feet above the lake, and Kyle offered her his hand. "Jump with me?"

"How deep is it?"

"In places about eighty feet, I am told. But it is safe enough to jump here."

Araceli linked hands with him and took a deep breath. "I'm trusting you."

Kyle had no idea how many times he'd made the same jump, but this time with Araceli it was a leap into something new and exciting.

And cold.

"Brrr! You could have warned me." Araceli shook her head, raining droplets of water around them.

"I prefer to think of it as refreshing." Kyle kicked out, leading Araceli across the pool to a large rock island. She followed using a strong sidestroke. Kyle scrambled out and helped Araceli up.

"Say cheese." He pointed to their driver across the way. Araceli laughed and waved. Kervens gave them a thumbs up and disappeared over the trail. They got back in the water. The only other group of people there had disappeared over by the waterfall into the pool below.

Araceli climbed back into the water and swam around the side of the rock, Kyle following. He found her floating on her back.

"Thanks for bringing me here. It's a little paradise. After seeing so much desperation, it is nice to see the land has a heart of hope."

Kyle joined her, linking his hand with hers as they floated. "I hadn't thought of this place that way, but you're right. It's like the smile on one of the kids' faces when they give you a hug, and I want to think for that child there is a brighter future." He changed to treading water and swam for a couple strokes. "Over here."

Araceli followed him to a natural underwater wall.

"Sit."

"This is weird. I feel like my legs are dangling over a precipice."

"Technically, you are." He studied her as she soaked in the beauty around them, the grotto-like setting protecting them from the rest of the world. He angled his body so he faced her. "Race you back to the waterfall?"

Araceli took off. He caught up as they neared the base. "You cheated."

She splashed him and swam off, and he chased her into one of the little crannies along the cliff face and splashed her back. She tried to get him, but he caught her hand and drew her close enough to see the flecks in her eyes reflecting the sunlight on the water. Marci's prompt came unbidden to his lips.

"*Ban m yon ti bo.*"

"What does that mean?"

"Kiss me."

For a moment they both froze, then Araceli put her free hand on his chest and pushed herself backward, widening the distance between them. "I am not sure I am ready to learn … but …" She brought her free hand to his cheek and bit her lip. "I think I want to."

The water swirled around him as she kicked herself forward and into his embrace. The meeting of their lips was too brief. Had they even touched? The necessity of treading water made it hard to hold her close and kiss her as he wished. He swam her farther into the crevice until his feet found a place to anchor. Araceli tucked a damp curl behind her ear. He wiped the moisture from her cheek and left his hand cupping her face. Then their eyes met, and Araceli's fluttered closed. She leaned forward to meet him.

"Ayyeee!" Splash.

Kyle pulled back and glanced over his shoulder at the intrusion to their paradise. Araceli said something under her breath he didn't quite catch above the yells of the boys cheering the diver on. Kyle turned back to her and dropped his hand from the side of her face where it still rested.

"Are you willing to take a rain check on that lesson in Creole?"

She blushed and nodded.

"Come on. It's time we headed back anyway."

The rain started to fall about an hour into the ride back to the guesthouse, slowing traffic. Araceli looked at Kyle's hand holding hers. It was the same hand that had cupped her face earlier. She hoped she wasn't blushing. At least her hair was hiding her face from Kyle. What must he think? The kiss she'd given him was no better than the ones her nephew had slobbered on her when he was one. If only those boys hadn't shown up.

Sure, she was blushing. She looked out the window to where the storm met the sea.

"A gourde for your thoughts?" Kyle smoothed the hair away from her face.

She didn't dare tell him what she was really thinking about. "I was wondering how many ships lie at the bottom of the ocean out there."

"No idea. Someone thought they found the *Santa Maria* some-place off the coast of Haiti, but it turned out to be another ship.

Tortuga, the famous pirate harbor, is on an island off the northern coast, so I am sure any number of ships sailed here. But I bet a gold doubloon that wasn't what you were really thinking about."

Araceli swung around to face him. "Why?" *Why do you have to be so close? You could have stayed in the other window seat rather than in the center. Why is my stomach turning little cartwheels? Why do I wish ill on five teenage boys?*

"Because you were blushing, and I find it hard to believe sunken treasure would make you blush."

"Oh."

"You are blushing again."

"And you are flirting."

"Yup."

Araceli turned back to the window.

Kyle leaned over until his chin hovered over her shoulder. "I want to spend more days with you. I know long-distance relationships don't have a good rap, but would you mind trying one with me? Perhaps after you graduate, we can figure out how to close the distance."

"You mean me find a job in Dallas?"

"Do you have a job lined up yet?"

"Not really. There was a job I applied for at the Boston Museum, but I haven't heard back from them. I thought I'd try what my roommate Candace does. She graduated and gets commissions to create various works, more on the illustration end, but it pays her bills. Or I could start a mural business. Then there's getting a job so I can save money for a master's."

"Art therapy?"

"Or a one-year teaching certification."

"If we can keep this working between us, could you look for something in the DFW area?"

"I think I can leave it as an option, but we haven't even known each other a week."

Kyle sat back in his seat. "Usually I wouldn't be talking about the future after a week either, but I don't know when we will get another semiprivate moment, and if our relationship is going to be more than a spring-break thing…"

Araceli pulled out her phone and handed it to Kyle. "I think this is where we exchange phone numbers. If this is going to work, I see a lot of texts and video calls in our future."

"I already have your info." Kyle typed his own contact information into her phone."

"How?"

"I have every volunteer's contact information in my phone— it's part of being over the trip."

She took her phone back. "There is nothing under *Kyle*."

"Try *menaj*. It is Creole for *boyfriend*."

"Really?"

"You can check your dictionary."

"That isn't what I meant."

He squeezed her hand. "It's your phone. If you think it's the wrong description, you're free to change it."

She slipped her phone back into her pocket.

"So, what am I in your phone?"

Kyle pulled out his phone and handed it to her.

Celi, ma belle.

twenty

EVERYONE WAS UP EARLY FOR their last day of work. Kyle was happy to see that most of the volunteers were still excited about being in Haiti and that the rain clouds hadn't dampened their spirits.

Tanner sat down with his breakfast. "Araceli, any ideas on what color to paint the cabinets?"

"The walls in the kitchen are yellow, right?"

His mouth full of pancake, Tanner nodded.

Araceli turned to Kyle. "Which would work better—traditional tan, brown, white, or something more fun and colorful, such as blue, red, or green?"

Marci spoke up. "I think you should go fun."

"Traditional makes the most sense," said Jade.

Everyone looked to Kyle.

"Why not something fun, but a lighter color so in the day when they are not using electricity it is easy to see indoors? The difficulty seeing indoors always bothered me about the old ones." Kyle hoped he was making the right choice. He knew nothing about interior decorating. And, admittedly, he may have chosen opposite Jade because he was still annoyed with her after last night. She'd given him no chance to slip away from the group for a private moment with Araceli, showing him every piece of artwork and every trinket she'd purchased. Then she'd monopolized Araceli by getting her professional opinion on each piece.

"Do you have enough paint left over from the walls, or do we need more?" asked Boyd.

"I used a flat paint on the walls. I'd use a semigloss on the cabinets, as that paint cleans up easier." Araceli took a bite of her muffin.

"Will it be possible to stop at the lumber supply on the way out?" asked Tanner.

Kyle checked his phone. "I need to meet with the director. Marci, can you go with that van? Tanner, Boyd, EmilyAnne, and Araceli, come with me. Everyone else go with Marci. Y'all can work on the yard cleanup while we wait. We concluded everyone was available to paint cabinets this morning, right?"

No one disagreed.

Outside, the vans honked for the gate to open.

Marci jumped up from her seat. "Last day! Let's make it awesome!"

Araceli wandered through the second-floor hallway. Every single clipboard was stuck firmly to the wall. The art gallery was done. Each child now had their own place to show off their artwork, schoolwork, or even a favorite picture out of one of the donated magazines. She fist pumped the air.

"Excited?"

"Kyle, I thought I was alone. Everyone was painting the cabinets or cleaning up."

"And how did you end up not doing either?" He stepped into her personal space.

She didn't retreat. Instead, she held up two paint brushes. "Supplies. And you?"

"I noticed you were missing and thought I should come find you."

"And now you have found me."

Kyle leaned in, but he only touched his lips to hers for a moment before pulling back. "Sadly, we need to go back before—"

"Kyle? Araceli? Tanner needs you!" The familiar voice carried up the stairs.

"Jade," they said in unison.

"There you two are." Jade looked from one to another, a frown forming between her eyebrows.

Araceli held up the brushes. "Apparently everyone needs to check up on me." She marched passed Jade and down the ramp. It wasn't hard to act annoyed. One day they would kiss without the fear of discovery.

Tanner waited on the back porch for the brushes. "Oh, these are perfect!"

Araceli took a brush and started on one of the unpainted cupboards. Jade and Kyle came out of the building. Kyle spoke to Tanner and left.

Jade picked up a brush and started painting the same cabinet as Araceli. In broad strokes, she painted the letters F-A-K-E across the wood. "I hope you have enjoyed your week here. We all think we will be different people when we get home. But after a couple of weeks, we're all the same again." She brushed more paint over the letters, obliterating them before moving on to a different cabinet.

"What did she want?" Madison started painting the cabinet to Araceli's left.

"To remind me of my place."

"Whatever she thinks it is, I suspect you are better off doing the opposite."

"True. I'm done with this one. I'm going to work on some doors." Araceli took her paint and moved to where the doors were laid out.

Kyle appeared with a paintbrush as she started the second door. "Interesting color choice. Reminds me of Bassin Bleu."

"I guess that was on my mind when I chose it."

"Any particular reason why?"

Araceli painted a long stroke down the door. "I don't know. I guess because it's pretty."

"The only reason?"

Araceli looked up from her work. How on earth did he paint in a clean T-shirt? "No, it is a color I want to remember."

"Me too."

"Glad to hear." She took her brush and tapped it on his shirt near the center of his chest.

"Hey!"

"It should be illegal to paint as much as you did this week and not have any on you. And now you can take some home with you." She grinned in triumph.

Kyle smiled back.

Araceli should have seen it coming, but the brush landed on her nose without warning.

"There. You marked your spot, and I marked mine."

Araceli tried to rub the paint off by rubbing her nose on her shoulder. "My spot?"

"Right over my heart. Even looks heart-shaped, in the biological sense."

"And my nose?"

Kyle leaned closer. "I couldn't kiss your little impertinent nose out here. And I didn't dare paint your lips."

"Oh." She scratched her nose with the back of her arm.

"And now you have smeared my mark all over your face." His smile was as big as the children's when they'd opened their Easter eggs.

Araceli's burning cheeks had nothing to do with the bright Haitian sun.

The last coat was finished before the volunteers broke out the protein bars and water for lunch, small groups of them going in search of shade. Several took refuge on the third-floor balcony. The breeze usually blew there, cooling it considerably.

"So, Marci, what's left to be done?" Kyle ripped open his protein bar, glad it was the last one he would eat for a while.

"We have the laminated photos of each child for them to put on their clipboards, and there will be a fashion show of the clothing made this week. After lunch they will install the cabinets and granite countertops Tanner found before the children get home from school. And Marlissa still needs to tell me her secret."

"So, what are you doing?"

"I'm going on baby-snuggling duty. Two of them are teething, and the aides are about worn out. Araceli, do you want to join me? I didn't drag you in with me earlier because you were so busy."

"No dragging necessary. Let me make sure most of this paint is off me."

Marci left with EmilyAnne and Araceli in tow.

Boyd set down his water bottle. "I see you finally got some paint on your shirt. It's about time. I was wondering if you were immune to dirt."

"Not immune. My Grandma Evans made me change clothes whenever she saw I was dirty. Then I would have to wash them. I hated doing laundry and became good at avoiding dirt."

"Your grandmother made you wash your own clothes? Didn't y'all have maids?"

"Mom employed a general cook and housekeeper, but she only worked four hours a day. Enough for Mom to work and stay on top of things. Dad really wanted us to have normal lives, and Mom agreed."

Boyd stuffed his trash in one of his pockets. "They did a good job. I'd never know you were born with a silver spoon. Ready guys? Countertops and plumbing await! Kyle, come stay clean helping us."

"I'll be there in a moment."

Kyle stopped by the director's office before going downstairs. "What have you learned?"

"I just got off the phone with Mrs. Deah. She found a doctor who's agreed to do Marlissa's surgery. Now we apply for a medical visa. I hope they give one to my wife, too. It will still be a few months before we can go, as this is a nonemergency procedure. But we will need to stay in the States for eight weeks. I have never left the orphanage for so long."

"I am sure Mom and I can come up with something. When do you think you will go?"

"July 10 is the day your mother set. We will need some help down here for a few months."

"Knowing Mom, that will be the day. We have been talking about hiring house parents for quite some time to help you. Maybe now is the time."

"Thank you for all your help this week. I am glad you were here so we could go to the doctor appointments."

"I assume this is the secret Marlissa has for Marci."

The director laughed. "Yes, she is so happy to get to go to America, I think she doesn't understand that she will be coming back to Haiti."

"I'll make sure Marci helps with that understanding."

Kyle hurried down the front stairway, stopping at the door to the nursery, where Araceli sang a French lullaby to the baby nestled on her shoulder. She turned and saw him watching and gave him a smile over the baby's head. His heart did a funny flip, his chest tightened, and for a moment he couldn't breathe.

Now he understood what Father was talking about when he told that ridiculous story about falling in love with Mom.

Music played from Chelsea's phone as the children strutted across the porch in their new clothes. Jade announced each child, saying something about their creation, as Marci interpreted. A couple of the dresses sewn by the older girls looked to Araceli's untrained eye to be more complicated. A few boys had sewn new shirts.

Everyone applauded when the last child twirled to show off her dress.

Saying goodbye to the children was going to be harder than she thought.

Tia gave her a huge hug and whispered, "It was Miss Jade. She said I would get in trouble if I told anyone. She said they would think I told lies and no one likes someone who lies."

Just as Araceli suspected. "Don't worry, I believe you. You are not in any trouble." Araceli hugged her again. There was no point in sharing Tia's revelation.

Martin tugged on her sleeve. "Miss Araceli, please come back and teach us about how to paint real things."

"I'll try." If things didn't work with Kyle, she didn't think she could ever come back. But if they did, maybe she could figure out how to come with the summer group.

"Try hard. We like you." André nodded to the children around them.

"I like all of you too." She blinked back tears.

Of all the other volunteers, only Marci seemed tearful. Marlissa's announcement about coming to Dallas for surgery had left the youngest Evans girl near tears all afternoon.

Half the volunteers had already climbed into the vans. Kyle and the director did their best to get the children, many of whom were still wearing their new clothes, away from the vans.

Kyle wrapped his arm around Araceli's waist. "Come on, ma belle. Time to go. Don't make it difficult on the children by letting them see your tears."

Araceli nodded and allowed herself to be led to the van. Kyle climbed in beside her. The doors slammed, and the drivers started back to the guesthouse.

The rutted roads didn't bother her as she watched children gather around the community well to draw water and listened to the colorful tap taps honk their horns. Marci was right about them. One could write a dictionary of the meanings of car horns in Haiti. Each beep and honk comprised a language the drivers understood.

Kyle's arm tightened around her shoulder. She hadn't realized he was holding her so close. She leaned into him and thought he kissed her hair. She wanted to say something but dared not miss any of the panorama outside the window.

"I forgot to buy something to take back to my roommates."

"We have a couple hours before we have to be at the airport in the morning. We will take y'all to a grocery store and an outdoor market. It will give you a chance to spend whatever leftover gourde you have from buying bottled water and dinner at the restaurant. Only the group that went to Labadee got any souvenirs, and I think the guys still need to buy their mothers something."

The smile in his voice brought a smile to her face.

"Thank you for a such an incredible week."

"Anytime."

If only.

twenty-one

LEAVING HAITI WAS MORE COMPLICATED than getting in. The customs officials questioned everyone no less than three times—the first time before they'd even checked in at the counter. Two full rounds of security scans were conducted—one to get onto the concourse and another to get off. The airport may have been able to fit onto a standard American football field, but they managed to put more security in the space than in the entirety of DFW.

Marci sat down next to Kyle on the hard plastic seats. "If you take EmilyAnne and me to the next concert of our choice, we will swap seats with you and Araceli so you can sit together."

Tempting. "Who else is in your row?"

Marci shrugged. "No one from our group."

"Floor seating or private box?"

"It depends on the concert."

"Deal."

Marci told him his new seat numbers. "We decided you could have the center and she gets the window."

"Good thinking." Considering he'd pondered upgrading to first class to have three more hours with Araceli, Marci's solution was perfect. Mostly because no one could complain he was playing favorites.

Araceli wandered back from the duty-free shops. "I found some of the Askanya chocolate you bought me in Jacmel. I probably bought more than I should, but my roommates and chocolate are inseparable. It will be gone by Sunday night." She took the seat Marci had vacated.

"My sister has been plotting. She and EmilyAnne are trading their seats for ours. They both end up with aisle seats, but we are together with a person not in our group in the third seat."

Araceli beamed. "She told me she was going to do it. How much did you have to pay her?"

"Tickets to an upcoming concert of their choice."

"I thought she would have tried for more."

"And I would have paid it."

They made their way through the last customs checks and out to the tarmac. Kyle made sure everyone got through security and on the plane before he boarded after Araceli."

They were just buckling in when they heard Jade and Marci arguing behind them. Kyle stood up and talked over the seats.

"Is there a problem, Jade? Is someone in your seat?"

"No. There is someone in your seat." Jade tilted her head in Marci's direction.

"Yes, I traded Marci her center seat for my aisle seat."

"What about Araceli?"

"She traded her aisle seat with EmilyAnne so Marci and EmilyAnne could still sit near each other. I am not sure how this affects your seat."

Jade crossed her arms and huffed. Marci sat down, and they avoided a scolding from a flight attendant.

Kyle also sat down and put on his seat belt. "I hope she doesn't give Marci a hard time, or I will have to up my payment."

Araceli smiled and took his hand in hers. "I hope it is worth it."

"It will be."

The fasten-seat-belt sign pinged for the last time. Araceli wished the flight wouldn't end. Even with a planned video call schedule and vague ideas of what she might do to find employment in Dallas, the next month and a half loomed large before them. But something in Kyle's eyes made her believe the promise that they could make the days apart work. He would fly into South Bend airport two days before graduation, and they would figure out things from there.

"What if I can't wait until mid-May to see you?" Kyle spoke in her ear.

"Last time I checked, both South Bend and Fort Wayne had daily flights to DFW. Or if you are really desperate, you can do what my old roommate's husband did and charter a flight to the county airport."

"How did he afford that?"

"Same way Daniel Crawford III affords anything, I suppose."

"The top-one-hundred most-eligible bachelor Daniel Crawford?"

Araceli smiled. "Yup, do you know him?"

"I've been at a benefit or two he has attended, but I don't really know him. How did she meet a billionaire?"

"Unlike us, they were friends when they were little." Araceli snuggled deeper into his chest. Ten more minutes and she wouldn't have the chance again.

"Wow, what are the chances two artists would date billionaires?"

"Three, maybe four. Not sure about the fourth. But they say opposites attract. Starving artist and never-gone-hungry billionaire. That is pretty opposite."

"Four?"

"Possibly. Tessa fell in love with Sean before he knew he was a billionaire, and he is having a hard time adjusting to all that money. He would be perfectly happy repairing organs for the rest of his life. He hasn't proposed yet. But he is building her a stained-glass studio near his home, so I think they are working on their happily ever after. Then there's Candace and Colin

Ogilvy, Daniel's best friend, who I am pretty sure is a billionaire. They have this odd friendship, both denying it's anything else. I am not so sure."

Kyle tightened his hold on her. "So, have you ever starved?"

"No, but I did clean bathrooms to raise part of the money to come until Mandy offered to sponsor me."

The pilot's voice came over the intercom announcing the standard prelanding instructions, the flight attendants translating them into French and Creole.

Kyle pulled his arm from around Araceli. "How long is your layover?"

She sat up but refused to let go of his hand. "Two hours. Long enough to get through customs, I hope."

"Ours is three. May I walk you to your terminal?"

"Of course."

Customs went faster than expected. The facial recognition machines helped. The group gathered their suitcases and checked in for the last leg of their flights. As she expected, her small plane to Fort Wayne was leaving from a different concourse than the flight to DFW. Araceli gave final hugs to most of the volunteers and promised to keep in touch with Madison and Marci as they waited to get through airport security, again.

"I don't think I have been scanned, sniffed, or inspected so much in my life. I feel as though I should get a sticker in the center of my forehead." Madison pointed to a place above her brows and crossed her eyes trying to look at it. "Inspected by number twelve and the K-9."

Everyone laughed as they boarded the trains to the terminals.

Kyle and Araceli got off first. He looked at the digital readout. "Thirty minutes until boarding. You don't have to sprint this time."

"Thank heavens."

They strolled behind the other passengers searching for their gates. As they started to pass an empty gate, Araceli led Kyle over to the window directly behind the check-in counter.

"This isn't your gate."

Araceli leaned her carry-on against the back side of the partition and spoke the words she had been practicing with the help of her translation app. *"Ban m yon ti bo?"*

Kyle cupped her face, and they enjoyed the first uninterrupted kiss of their relationship. Araceli went up on her tiptoes to deepen the connection. Kyle's arm encircled her waist, securing it.

It was over too soon.

Kyle rested his forehead on hers. "I wonder if there are any seats left on your plane."

"Deah might not be too happy if you don't go home with Marci."

"But she would be thrilled to know I am in love."

Araceli pulled her head back so she could look into his eyes. "Are you?" She was as helpless to stop the grin on her face as she was the heat in her cheeks.

"Aren't you?"

She pulled him into an answering kiss. She didn't dare say the words, hoping it would be answer enough for now.

Above their heads, the loudspeaker crackled.

This time Araceli ended the kiss. "My flight."

Kyle leaned down and took her bag in one hand and her hand in the other.

At the gate, he pulled her into a hug, and they waited until everyone else boarded. His last kiss was to the tip of her nose. "Fly safe, Celi, ma belle."

She didn't look back as she walked down the Jetway. If she did, she knew she would not get on the plane.

twenty-two

CANDACE LOOKED AT HER PHONE. "It is almost eight. Are you going to your room or hogging Lover's Loft again?"

"I am not hogging it. You and Zoe don't need to use the loft, and since Tessa is in New York 'setting up her studio,' she isn't using it." Araceli felt snarky enough to use air quotes. "Do you really have a problem while I talk on the phone up there? It isn't like when Sean is here, or Daniel was last year. Believe me, I really am just looking at the stars."

Zoe looked up from her laptop. "You know we are teasing you, and Candace is worried about having to find a new roommate. Although Abbie has taken Tessa's room and will be hanging around until the baby is born since she doesn't like hanging around with the other guards when her brother isn't one of them. That still leaves Candace with empty rooms."

"It isn't like you are losing me because of Kyle. I'm still graduating."

"But if you chose more education, you would be here another year." Candace twirled the ends of the orange paisley scarf she wore.

Araceli's phone chimed for an incoming video call, and she sprinted to the library before answering.

"Hello?"

"Celi, ma belle, how are you this evening? Ready for your Haitian lesson?" Kyle started the call as he always did.

Araceli settled into one of the beanbags in the loft. After two weeks of nightly calls, she felt as if their relationship was growing stronger.

"I can't come out next weekend to celebrate your birthday like I planned." Kyle's frustration filled the screen.

"What happened? Not your grandfather, I hope."

"No. Jade's dad pulled some strings and got us on one of the weekend Dallas shows. Mom has never taken the plight of the Haitians to TV before, but she feels the timing is right. Since they are featuring our last trip, they want me or Marci on the show."

"And everyone wants to keep Marci out of the media as long as possible." Araceli finished the thought for him.

"What about the next weekend?"

"We talked about that one. It's the weekend before all my final projects are due. As much as I want you here, I won't get anything done."

"Nothing? I am sure we would do something."

Araceli made a face. "You know what I mean."

A chime went off on Kyle's side of the phone. "Our two hours are up."

"Seriously hate the phone-call curfew."

"And I hate it when you miss class because we talk until 3:00 a.m."

Araceli sat up. "And you fall asleep in some meeting."

"Night Celi, ma belle."

"Ou toujou nan kè mwen."

Kyle smiled. "You are always in my heart too."

The screen went dim. Araceli blew a kiss to the sky. Maybe it would find him.

Kyle wasn't sure what had happened between the conversation in the green room with the show's host, former Miss Texas Amanda Lamb, and the live filming. Somehow Jade had commandeered the entire show, including the seat next to Amanda, where he was supposed to be sitting. Every time he opened his mouth to answer a question, Jade responded first. At least she had her facts straight on poverty, human trafficking, and orphanages in general.

When they started showing slides of the trip, Kyle looked for Marci in the audience. When he found her, he shook his head. Whatever Marci was planning was foolish and rash and probably involved storming the stage.

Marci's jaw dropped. Kyle redirected his attention to the slides. The photo currently on the screen showed Jade holding a paintbrush and pretending to paint on the crack in the wall, surrounded by children. Before he could interrupt, they moved on to the next slide showing the men working on the cabinets.

One of the handprint-animal walls flashed on the screen. Jade continued to narrate. "The children loved helping with this wall. They were so sweet. Their smiles would warm your heart."

Kyle fumed. Jade hadn't even been there.

"Perhaps Mr. Evans would like to—" Amanda tried to cut in.

Jade patted his knee. "Oh, this slide is of the men repairing damage to the roof caused by the last hurricane."

Kyle moved Jade's hand. The slides ended.

"I have enough time for a couple questions from the audience." Amanda shaded her eyes and pointed to one of the plants with a prescreened question.

"My question is for Mr. Evans. Why do you work so hard down there and raise funds when you could use your family fortune to pump money into Haiti?"

Kyle leaned forward in the chair. "That is really a three-part question. One of the major reasons we don't just send money ties into the lessons learned from the 2010 earthquake."

"One more question." Again, Amanda pointed to a prearranged plant.

"This question is for Jade. Is it true you are engaged to Mr. Evans?"

That was not the question about child slavery he was expecting.

Jade was talking and tugging at his hand. Kyle turned to correct her. But as he did, Jade lunged into his arms and planted a kiss on him before he could push her off.

Amanda signaled the camera crew to focus in on her. "Thank you, Evans Foundation, for making a difference in the world. Be sure to stay tuned for Sports Saturday and, as always, y'all have a safe and wonderful weekend!"

Finally, someone yelled, "And cut!"

Kyle stormed off the stage knowing Jade would follow. He didn't want to air this conversation in front of shocked audience members or cameras. Her heels clicked behind him.

He turned and put his hands up to keep her from coming closer. "Stop. Not. Another. Step. I am not sure what happened out there, but it was not what I planned. And in case I didn't make myself clear in any of our previous conversations, I am never going to marry you. Not even if it would magically save Haiti."

The other volunteers, Marci, Amanda, and her producer stood inside the doorway watching the drama unfold.

"I don't care what Grandfather's PR firm comes up with to fix your little stunt, you will comply. And then I never want to see you again, and, if necessary, I will get a restraining order." He knew he was going too far and letting anger cloud his words. He looked to Marci. "Get a ride with EmilyAnne. I need to go clear my head."

Kyle climbed in the cab of his truck and turned the ignition.

How would he explain this to Araceli?

twenty-three

THEY ALL STARED AT THE screen in silence.

Zoe shut off the webcast. "Maybe there was more we didn't see when they cut to the commercial."

Araceli tried to swallow the lump in her throat. It sat there like a too-big vitamin.

Mandy handed Araceli more tissues. "Hey, there could be another explanation. Like when Summerset Vandermark set Daniel up."

Araceli's phone beeped. She read Tessa's text. **That kiss was soooo fake. Talk to him. Don't write him off.** She handed the phone to Abbie, who read the text to everyone.

Her phone beeped again. Marci. **Kyle yelled at Jade and left. They are not engaged. REPEAT: NOT ENGAGED. I have his phone in my purse. Don't dump him. Please!!!** The text ended in several emojis, mostly hearts.

"I am not upset about the kiss. I spent a week as Jade's roommate. Of course she set it up. Why does everyone assume I am upset about the kiss?"

Candace put an arm around Araceli. "Because that is when you started crying."

"I did not."

One painted-on eyebrow raised high enough to touch Candace's wig.

Mandy stood. "Anyone want ice cream? I have a new double-chocolate caramel brownie."

Maybe it would numb the pain for a moment. Araceli raised her hand along with the others. Abbie followed Mandy into the kitchen.

A text from Cassie, whom she only met on video calls. **My brother is an idiot. I'll go knock some sense into him as soon as I get home from Paris.**

Araceli wasn't sure what to reply, so she set the phone down.

"So, if it wasn't the kiss, why are you so upset?" Mandy handed Araceli an overflowing bowl of ice cream.

"The kiss was more like the last straw. Part of me knows he wasn't enjoying it, and he was pushing back, but I still saw a kiss. But it was his not correcting Jade on the painting. She helped all of ten minutes and tried to destroy the mural, not that I ever told him that. But the photo they showed looked like she was directing everything. Even when the host complimented Jade on all her work, Kyle didn't correct her. I didn't expect Chelsea would because she is Jade's sidekick, but Kyle didn't take the opening." Araceli took a too-large bite, hoping for the pain from an ice cream headache to dull the other pain.

Mandy sat on Araceli's other side. "Nonartists don't understand how much of our souls we put into the work. Having someone not credit you when credit is due is almost as bad as having your work plagiarized."

"Try graphic design. No one ever gives you credit unless it is a logo." Zoe crossed her arms.

Araceli wiped her tears. "I thought we already established that graphic artists don't do art. You don't take the photos, draw the illustrations, create the font, or write the copy. So, since you don't do anything, you don't need the credit." She flashed Zoe a big smile so Zoe would know it was all teasing.

"Hey! From what you say, even I do more than Jade did. At least I put the credits in for the artists and writers." Zoe made a face and stuck out her tongue. There was no way a designer would ever win the argument in a house full of artists.

Abbie moved a pillow out of the way. "If you want, I can send Alex out to have words with Kyle."

Mandy nodded. "Alex is in desperate need of something with a bit more action than following a woman who is starting to wobble."

"Thanks for the offer, but I'll pass. I don't want to force him to apologize."

"Are you at least going to explain how much he hurt you?"

Araceli shrugged. "I don't know if I can. You guys get me because you are artists. What if he doesn't?"

"I don't think you need to be an artist to empathize with having the credit given to someone else. I've had others claim my ideas before, and it hurts. After all the hard work you did at the orphanage, I think it would hurt more than having someone take credit for a suggestion." Abbie's thoughts were unexpected. She usually stayed on the fringes of their conversations. The distinction between bodyguard and friend blurred more each day.

"You told me he was smart. I bet you a week's worth of household duties he gets it within the next four hours and you get a call." Zoe extended her hand for a handshake.

"I'll double that." Candace added her hand.

"If I lose, do I have to do your work?"

Zoe and Candace conferred silently. "No."

"Okay, then, at least if he doesn't call I get out of some cleaning."

Mandy set her empty bowl on the coffee table. "More ice cream?"

Candace picked up the empty bowl. "Wow, you really are eating for two. You didn't eat that much ice cream when you were upset with all of Daniel's fake dates."

"Doctor's orders. I lost too much weight the first trimester. Ice cream equals calcium and calories, not to mention its magical qualities of soothing broken hearts."

"I think I would feel better if I could throw it at Kyle, or perhaps Jade." Araceli put the last spoonful in her mouth.

"If you do, make sure it isn't the good stuff. Use bubble-gum or cotton-candy ice cream. They might even stain."

Everyone laughed at Zoe's suggestion.

Araceli took a deep breath. "Don't we have a nursery to paint?"

Welcome to Oklahoma!

Kyle sped past the sign and glanced at the clock on his dashboard—two and a half hours since he'd left the news station. His only thought was to get to Celi. Odd his sisters hadn't called him to ask where he went. Mom should have called by now too. He didn't expect Celi to call, not after the disaster of a show.

He felt for his phone on the console.

Oh no.

A few choice words ran through his brain. He'd put his phone in Marci's purse when they were in the green room getting ready for the show. Turning around would add at least five hours to the trip as traffic would have picked up by now and the construction areas would be clogged to a standstill. Even if he found a flight, he wouldn't make it before tomorrow morning.

He passed the casino on the south side of Durant, and the highway traffic immediately diminished. His truck's GPS told him there were twelve more hours of driving. By the time he turned around, purchased a plane ticket, transferred, and rented a car, he would have used twelve hours anyway. But Mom would go only slightly crazy if he didn't call until tomorrow morning, so he pulled off the highway and found a Walmart not far from a Chicken Express.

Setting up his burner phone while eating fried chicken required more napkins than he anticipated. Before leaving, he paid for a double order of rolls and fried pickle slices to go—comfort food for the road as the gravy would be too messy to eat and drive.

In the truck, he connected the phone to his hands-free speakers. "Okay, Google. Call Marci."

The female computer voice responded, "Who do you want to call?"

Kyle looked at the screen and repeated, "Marci."

The voice responded, "I do not know Marci. Please try again."

No phone numbers. Why hadn't he memorized anything other than his parents' landline and his office number? He punched in the number to the home phone, grateful the number hadn't changed since kindergarten. Predictably, his call went to voice mail. "Hi, Mom, Marci has my phone. I am going to Indiana. I need to … I need to … Please have Marci call me at …" Kyle paused. He didn't know his new number. "At whatever Oklahoma number is on the caller ID. I got a burner. Love y'all. Bye."

Before getting back on the highway, Kyle filled the tank with gas. It crossed his mind that he could video call as he knew the passwords. But he needed to hold Celi, and a call wasn't the same. What he wanted to do was kiss her silly to erase Jade's kiss and tell her in person…What *was* he going to say to her? He had no idea. But something had clicked halfway through the interview. Celi wasn't there, and it was wrong.

Four hours later, he crossed into Missouri and Marci finally called.

"What are you doing?" She didn't even say hello.

"Driving to Indiana."

"Either this is the most romantic thing ever or you are stupid!"

"Why do you say I am stupid?"

"Have you called her?"

"Of course not. My phone is in your purse."

"See? Stupid. It has been six hours since you left here, and what do you think she has been doing? Waiting for you to call!"

"I don't have her number." Kyle could feel Marci's eye roll over the phone.

"Do you even have a plan? Or are you going to show up at 3:00 a.m. and wing it?"

"Pretty much. And apologize for the kiss and Jade's announcement."

"You are stupid, bro. I doubt she is as upset by the kiss as she is by what you said, or *didn't* say, during the interview." He pictured Marci rolling her eyes at him again.

"What are you talking about?"

Marci huffed before answering "The part where you agreed Jade was a great painter."

"I what?"

"You weren't paying attention, were you?"

"The whole thing was distracting. Nothing went as planned. I was thinking and trying to stay out of Jade's reach after they sat us on the couch together."

"Poor big brother. So much on his mind he didn't know what he was saying." Sarcasm oozed through the speaker.

"Hey, I was on top of things. I described Mom's work and the difficult situation down there without sounding like a bleeding heart or an unfeeling politician."

"You have practiced it enough you should have, but then you totally spaced when they started showing the photos."

"They showed the photo of Celi with the paint on her face, and I got distracted. She should have been there. I heard from the director that the children love having their own spaces to show off their art and work. Even some of the kids about to age out are using their spaces. A couple of the ones experiencing problems in school worked harder so they'd have papers to put in their clips."

"Have you told Araceli you wanted her there?"

"Not in so many words."

"Sheesh, you are an idiot. Where are you, anyway?"

"I just passed Joplin."

"Hey, isn't that like Route 66?"

"I'm on the freeway, but I did see a few signs. I think they overlap."

"So how many hours do you have left?"

Kyle read his GPS. "About eight or nine."

"Then you have time to show up with something better than flowers!"

He needed *way* more than flowers. Tomorrow was Celi's birthday. He'd already sent her gift, but if he was going to be there ...

Before he could ask Marci anything else, the connection was lost.

Kyle couldn't call back using voice commands because the number wasn't in his contacts. At least he had Marci's phone number now. He pulled off at the next exit. There was only one number listed in his history. Marci had called from the landline. He called it anyway.

It went to voice mail.

"Marci, please text me Celi's number."

"Here is one more paintbrush." Zoe dropped the blue-tinged brush in the sink where Araceli was cleaning the other brushes they'd used to paint the nursery.

The grandfather clock chimed six, and the doorbell rang.

"That better be the pizza. I am starving." Mandy didn't bother answering the door. Either Alex or Abbie would. As long as there wasn't a security gate on the house and grounds, it was one of the things Mandy couldn't do.

Alex came in, arms full of pizza boxes. "You do realize you should have asked me to go pick these up, right? I had to run to intercept him at the door."

Mandy opened the top box. "Sorry, I didn't think about it at the time."

"Can you at least pretend to let me earn my pay?"

"Sure, you can deck the next man to come to the door."

"You do realize your husband should be here within the hour?"

Mandy bit her lip. "Okay, the next person who isn't my husband—as long as you take one of those lots-a-meat pizzas back over to the garage with you."

"Only for you, Mrs. Crawford." Alex slid the two bottom boxes out of the pile and went out the back door in the direction of the detached garage with its attic apartment that doubled as a security center.

Candace snagged a piece of the veggie pizza. "I thought Daniel wasn't coming until the morning."

"He called me a couple hours ago when you and Araceli were debating if the gray was too cool to paint the entire room in. By the way, I am glad she won. I think the stripes are perfect."

Candace twirled the end of her headscarf. "Is he alone?"

"Of course not. He will have Mr. Hastings with him. But that isn't what you are asking, is it, cousin?" Zoe's voice was teasing.

Candace joined Araceli at the sink, her back to the room. A faint blush tinted her cheeks, but Araceli knew better than to tread where Zoe dared. Teasing Candace about Colin could land a girl homeless.

"I think you both owe me a week of household chores. It has been more than four hours."

"Make sure you give Zoe the worst ones. How are you doing?"

"Fine, as long as I don't think. I am glad we decided to paint the nursery today. I don't think I could have concentrated on my end-of-term paper for English."

"Three weeks until graduation. How do you feel?"

"Confused? I applied to a couple Dallas-area universities, but I need to pick up some classes someplace for prerequisites if I want to become an art therapist."

"So you decided?"

"I thought so. I applied for jobs in the DFW area. Deah says the kids at the orphanage love their gallery and it is helping some of them express themselves. She jokes they may go through half the donated crayons before the end of the year if they don't run out of paper first. They are working on convincing them to use both sides."

Candace wrapped the bristles of a brush in a paper towel. "So, what are you going to do this summer?"

Araceli shrugged. Friday night, Kyle had discussed the possibility of going to Haiti in July and being house parents for three months. They'd danced around the notion that the directors who served as house parents were married and shared a little apartment on the top floor. There was a separate bedroom up there one of them could use. This assumed the board would approve it in the first place. The conversation had served as the catalyst for her dreams last night and daydreams this morning. All shattered by the reality of the TV.

"Hey, are you two going to come eat?" Zoe asked around the food in her mouth.

Still unwilling to answer Candace's question, Araceli grabbed a paper plate and joined the others at the table.

twenty-four

IT WAS PAST SUNSET BY the time Kyle reached St. Louis. Despite stops at three different roadside gift/tourist traps, he was making decent time. He'd picked up several Askinosie chocolate bars, similar enough to the Askanya chocolate they'd purchased in Haiti for his purposes, as well as a custom-made teddy bear sewn from old jeans with a working pocket. The "I'm in Missouri without you" T-shirt seemed like a good idea an hour ago. Not so much now.

Marci hadn't called back.

While putting together a gas-station dinner, Kyle called home again.

Deah answered. "Kyle, is that you?"

"Ya, is Marci there?"

"No, and you need to explain yourself."

Kyle added an energy drink to the assortment of things in his arms. "I'm in a gas station on the outskirts of St. Louis buying a high-caffeine dinner."

"Why are you on this road trip?"

"At the time, driving over to DFW and catching the first flight to Fort Wayne or South Bend and renting a car didn't enter my mind. So I just drove."

"Kyle Alan Evans! That is not what I mean, and you know it." His mother's voice boomed through the phone.

"Mom, I know what you mean. But I am not going to explain myself in a gas-station convenience store. Let me check out. Did Marci get my message? She hasn't texted me Celi's number."

"I don't know. She went to the movie."

"Do you have Celi's number?"

"Yes."

"Will you text it to me?" Kyle set his food on the counter.

"Possibly, after I get some answers."

Kyle gave the clerk his credit card and a tight smile.

The clerk handed him a receipt but no bag.

"I'll call you back in a minute, Mom." Kyle put the phone in his pocket and stacked his purchases in his arms. After he got in the truck, he redialed home.

Voice mail?

Kyle hung up without leaving a message. No way was he going to leave a message that could come back to haunt him or be misunderstood.

Abbie accompanied the roommates back to the house. The apartment above the garage was crowded with just her and Alex. Add her father and the other security men traveling with them, and it was uncomfortably small. With Colin staying in the Crawford's guest room, Mr. Hastings had given her the night off to go find more suitable accommodations.

Araceli was more than happy for the extra company. With Tessa in New York again, she needed the buffer between the cousins and their questions.

However, the bodyguard did not keep Candace from following Araceli into her bedroom. "Spill it. You've managed to avoid me since the pizza came."

"I wasn't about to say anything during Mandy's reveal party. The look on Daniel's face when he unwrapped boxes and boxes of pink! Did you know?"

"I don't even think Abbie knew. Mandy must have ordered everything online. I know Daniel was upset he couldn't be there for the ultrasound. This mess with the company in China has had him tied in knots. I am glad it is over." Candace moved a pile of things from the chair and took a seat.

"How does Colin feel about it?"

"Relieved. Anytime they divest the company of one of their father's interests, Colin always feels like a weight has been lifted. I think he would be happier if he had about a tenth of the income he has."

"If he did, he would be living in his mother's basement, hacking into the DOD, CIA, or MI6."

"You mean as opposed to sitting in his penthouse and hacking?"

"I was joking. He doesn't, does he?"

"Not since he was a teenager. I think the only thing that saved him was his father's connections."

"No way!" Araceli moved a couple of her piles, keeping an eye on the one Candace had moved. She knew her roommate would never believe she was organizing and dejunking.

"Have I let you distract me long enough? I asked what you were going to do this summer, and you got a very peculiar look on your face. So tell."

Araceli held up her hands. "Right now I don't know. Last night I was making plans to go back to Haiti for three months to be a house mom at the orphanage."

"And who was going to be the house dad?"

"Kyle."

Candace jumped out of her seat. "Are you engaged?"

"No, we kind of danced around that part of the arrangement. And before you ask anything embarrassing, there is no way we would live together and not be married, especially at the orphanage, but there are some options where we wouldn't be sharing the apartment."

"Do you want to be?"

Araceli shuffled the papers from her freshman year headed for the recycle bin. "I did, but I don't know. What if I am making another one of my flighty decisions? What if I'm not really in love?"

"Do you think you are in love?" Candace pulled off her wig and fixed the strands.

"I don't know. I like him. He is amazing with the kids, and when he is at fault, he owns up to it. Well, until today. Today he is off-grid. I texted Marci when you were hanging the pink curtains. She still has his phone and couldn't tell me where he was other than 'out driving.'" Araceli added air quotes for emphasis. "He has been gone for nearly twelve hours. I know Texas is a big place, but I'm worried. What if he drove off the road and met a rabid armadillo or something?"

Candace drew Araceli into a hug. "I don't think you need to worry about a rabid armadillo. More likely one of the suicidal skunks they have down there. In some places, you can't drive more than five miles without finding one in the road. Especially in the spring."

"Have you been to Texas?"

Candace stepped back. "A few times. Mom and I spent time at MD Anderson in Houston. The flight made Mom so sick she made Dad drive down there. That was when we took the photo of us in the bluebonnet field. We were lucky they only bloom in March. Don't ever tell, but I picked one for my scrapbook."

"Why would I tell?"

"For years I heard it was illegal to pick the state flower, but it isn't. At the time, I did it because I wanted to be a bit of a delinquent. I think part of me wanted to be arrested. But who was going to give a ticket to the teenager puking her guts up after chemo? One look at Mom and I and the officer might have picked us a huge bouquet."

"The photo you have hanging above your bed, isn't it."

"Yup. The last family photo. Mom and I in our brand-new wigs. My sister caked makeup on both of us. But it turned out nice. I think Mom knew when she planned the session it might be the last one."

Araceli didn't know what to say. It wasn't often Candace opened up about her life. It was no big secret she was a cancer survivor. She was one of those rare people who'd acquired a chemotherapy-induced Alopecia that remained for nearly a decade. Candace had embraced the condition with bright, outrageous wigs and the occasional scarf in public. Around the house, she would often go au natural, especially in the studio. But she rarely spoke of her mother, who'd passed away from complications from her cancers.

"Sorry, I didn't mean to—"

Araceli cut Candace off. "You didn't. I needed the perspective for a moment. I have been a bit too deep in my own head today. It is worth waiting for Kyle to contact me before I go back to talking to my teddy-bear boyfriends."

"You would have to dig them out anyway." Candace gestured to the pile in the corner. "But for what it is worth, since I have only met him by video call, I think he is good for you."

"I kind of think so too." At least she hoped so. Seeing Mandy and Daniel tonight reminded her that having patience to work through things was the better course of action.

Kyle's glimpse of the Gateway Arch as he turned to cross over the Mississippi and into Illinois wasn't enough. He added visiting the landmark to his bucket list. His phone rang.

"What is this about you driving a thousand miles for a girl? You know, when I was your age, there was this song about walking five hundred miles for a girl."

"I know, Dad. There are some great covers for the song. Marci listens to one of them daily."

"So what are your intentions, exactly?"

"I know it's fast, but I have been seriously thinking marriage."

"How seriously?" His father's voice lost the joking tone.

"Driving-sixteen-hours-across-the-country-to-apologize serious."

"You should know Rich Williams called me awhile ago."

"Celi's dad? Why did he call you?"

"He watched the video of this morning's interview. He wanted to know if you were going to break his daughter's heart. You know how I felt about the idiot doctor who dated Cassie?"

"The one you wanted to report to the ethics committee for violating the 'first do no harm' thing?"

"I wanted to do more, but that was the only thing I could legally do. Well, Rich feels the same about you at the moment. If you are considering a proposal, I think you need to get his blessing pronto. Is there a place you can pull over?"

Kyle looked for an exit and saw a green sign. "There is an exit in two miles."

"Then I'll text you his number. Don't delay. It's an hour later there."

"Will you text me Celi's number, too?"

"Not until you get Rich's blessing."

Of course. But at some point he needed her number or he wasn't going to be able to find her when he did get to Indiana. "Thanks, Dad."

The next BP gas station beckoned. Kyle parked the truck and took a deep breath before dialing the number his father had sent.

"Hello, Mr. Williams? This is Kyle Evans."

twenty-five

AT 4:20 A.M. EASTERN TIME, Kyle pulled into a Walmart parking lot five miles from the art college. This was as close as he could get without an address. Rich Williams had refused to provide his daughter's address, telling Kyle to think of it as a test of his dedication. Apparently, driving 1,087 miles was not enough.

Even if he knew Celi's location, he couldn't go there now. He had left without even a toothbrush and dribbled cola down his shirt near Kokomo. Kyle had never had much cause for twenty-four-hour shopping, but he couldn't be more thankful for the bright lights of the supercenter. As he got out of his truck and headed for the door, a structure off to the side caught his eye. It looked like a vast, empty carport. It must be the Amish parking Celi had told him about in one of their phone chats. He'd noticed the buggy caution signs as he'd gotten off the main highway.

Kyle loaded his basket with travel-sized toiletries, two shirts, and more energy drinks than was strictly healthy, then he wandered down the snack aisle looking for sunflower seeds and anything crunchy for the drive home. His first meeting wasn't until 11:00 a.m. on Monday, but it was a client he could not skip out on. The drive back would be brutal. He could fly and have his truck shipped, but a Texan just didn't leave his truck.

This early on a Sunday morning, only a few picked-over flowers remained in the display. Thankfully, a couple of the bouquets looked more alive than dead. If he combined them, he could get a decent-looking bunch. He was glad he followed Marci's advice and picked up the chocolate and denim bear. Still, it didn't seem like he had quite the right things, so he wandered around the aisles looking for something to round out his gift.

It wasn't perfect and cost less than twenty dollars, but if they were going to be in Haiti for three months, she would want it. Kyle debated between two different styles, choosing the one with the delicate curve. Guessing the right size was another problem. Hopefully Marci's size would work.

The sleepy-eyed cashier looked up when he came to the last item on the belt—the flowers. "Man, I'd at least wait until sunrise before you give her these."

"I plan to." Kyle paid and went to brush his teeth.

Araceli glared at her phone. 7:10. Why would Mandy be calling?

"Hey, Mandy, what's up?"

"We had a security breach, and ..." Mandy paused while she laughed. "And, I think you need to get over here." Mandy's laughter came again. "Remember last night when I told Alex he could hit the next guy who came to the door?"

Tossing the covers off, Araceli sat up and rubbed her face. "Over the pizza delivery."

"Alex wants a reason why not to hit this trespasser again. After yesterday, you get the final say."

"Is this a pregnancy thing? You aren't making any sense."

Mandy was laughing so hard she couldn't answer for a minute. Araceli stood and tossed her pillows back on her bed while she waited. Finally, Mandy spoke. "Kyle is here."

Araceli shook her head. "What did you say?"

"Kyle is here."

The bed spring creaked as Araceli collapsed onto it. "How? Why?"

"How? He drove here. Apparently you mentioned I lived behind the Crawford Family Community Center, and he didn't have your phone number or address. As for why, you will need to ask Kyle. How soon can you be here?"

The reflection in her mirror begged for at least an hour to tame her bedhead. "Give me twenty minutes."

"Okay, see you in twenty."

"And, Mandy, don't let Alex hit Kyle until I talk with him!" Araceli ran to the bathroom.

Abbie met her in the hall. "My father called. There has been an incident at the house, and I am to drive you up there as soon as you are ready."

"I know. Mandy called. Give me fifteen."

Araceli shut the bathroom door to the sound of Abbie's laughter.

Twelve and half minutes later, Araceli watched out the window as Abbie hurried her truck along the quiet streets. Few ventured out this early on a Sunday.

Abbie's phone beeped, and she tapped the Bluetooth in her ear. Her one-word answers gave no clue as to the conversation, but from the quick glance Abbie gave her, Araceli was sure someone was discussing her. Abbie drove past the road they usually took to Mandy's and the Crawford mansion, turning on the next street down.

"Where are we going?"

"The back gate to the old property. Daniel still owns much of the land, including the pond. They wanted me to drop you off at the gazebo overlooking the pond."

"What is going on?"

"You know as much as I do." Abbie turned the car into a security gate and pushed a button above the mirror. The gate opened for them. She drove to the end of the road, where Alex stood, arms crossed, next to a truck with Texas plates.

When Abbie parked, Alex came over and opened the passenger-side door, then handed Araceli a whistle. "Mandy made me promise to stay here, but if anything goes down, you yell or use this. I'll be over the hill faster than Usain Bolt running the two hundred in the Olympics."

Araceli lifted the whistle in a salute and headed up the path.

Alex called after her. "And the bruise on his cheek was an accident!"

Okay, then ... Araceli bit her lip and continued up the path.

The ducks startled at the sound of car doors slamming. Kyle turned his attention to the top of the hill. As soon as he saw Celi, he wanted to run to her like some old movie or cheesy commercial. Instead, he walked. A breeze caught some of her hair from her messy bun, making it dance in front of her face. She tucked it behind her ear only to have the wind catch it again.

Kyle hurried his next few steps. As he took the errant strand of hair in his fingers, everything he'd rehearsed fled on the breeze. He didn't have words. She was there, the faint smell of her citrus shampoo or lotion filling the air around him with the essence he hadn't realized he missed for the past three weeks until he smelled it again. He smoothed the hair behind her ear and let his hand linger, cupping her head, his thumb tracing the top of her cheekbone.

As she looked him in the eye, he thought he saw a thousand unanswered questions. Keeping his hand on the side of her head, he moved closer. Celi's eyes fluttered closed, and he tried to answer all of her questions with a kiss. But the first brush was not enough. Neither was the second. He moved his other hand to her waist and pulled her closer. Celi matched his next kiss with answers of her own.

Kyle pulled back and rested his forehead against hers. "I was going to start by giving you flowers and apologizing for yesterday. I got thinking about you in the interview, wishing you were there. I didn't realize until I watched it on my phone this morning how it looked and sounded. I was such a jerk not to correct the host, and then Jade and the kiss. And then—"

A finger on his lips stopped him. "You brought me flowers?"

He kissed the finger. "It is your birthday. And I brought you chocolate and a bear but no cake."

Kyle stepped back and took Celi's hand.

"Oh, he is adorable!" Celi dropped Kyle's hand and picked up the denim bear. "Where did you find him?"

"At this quilt-and-souvenir shop in the Ozarks. The chocolate was from another shop near Springfield. The flowers are from the Walmart down the road. I thought of getting you something from every state, but by the time I thought of it, I'd already missed Oklahoma, unless you want my burner phone. And all the roadside shops were closed in Illinois other than the gas stations. And somehow getting you a coffee cup touting 'The land of Lincoln' didn't seem romantic." Kyle knew he was rambling, but he couldn't stop as he led her down to the gazebo.

Celi played with the bear's ears. "I can't believe you drove here. Isn't that like a thousand miles?"

Kyle nodded. He would drive a thousand more.

The flowers lay on the table in the center of the gazebo. Araceli picked them up to smell them again. Underneath lay gray fabric. She picked up the shirt. "What is this?"

Kyle blushed a full-on blush. "Um, something that seemed perfect last evening that looks rather stupid in the light of day.

She read the shirt twice. "What a terrible pun. 'Missouri without you.' Were you?"

Kyle moved closer, and Araceli stepped into his arms. "Both literally and figuratively. Marci wouldn't give me your number, so I couldn't even call. But it gave me time to think."

"About what?" She picked up the bear again. He would be so perfect for her collection. She didn't have anything like him.

"About the fact that I should have driven to DFW and flown—gas prices go up as you get farther from Texas. And about how Indiana has really odd names, like Miami, Nead, and Tippecanoe—that last one is funny. I imagined a couple of different ways it got its name. And about how your father isn't as scary as I think he pretends to be. And about how I have to be back in Irving by 11:00 am tomorrow. But mostly about you and us and things."

Us. The word echoed inside Araceli's head. Us felt right. *Dad isn't scary? Wait, what?* She looked up to ask him at about the same time she felt something hard in the pocket that covered the bear's chest. It felt like … No. It couldn't be.

Araceli pulled a silver ring out of the pocket.

And Kyle was down on one knee. "I know this ring doesn't have a real diamond, but it doesn't mean what I feel isn't real. Araceli Williams, will you be my wife?"

Tears formed, but unlike the ones she'd indulged in late last night, these were welcome tears. "Yes. Yes!" Her shout was loud enough to disturb the ducks in the pond. As Kyle stood, she launched herself into his arms, igniting a kiss that confirmed her acceptance of his proposal.

Kyle pulled back before one kiss melted into ten. "Let me put it on your finger." He slipped the ring on her finger.

"You talked to my dad?"

"From St. Louis to Effingham, Illinois. He said he would consider giving his blessing if you convinced him you really want me."

Araceli grabbed the front of his shirt. "I do." She kissed him again.

The pounding of footsteps interrupted them, and Kyle stiffened.

"I told you so." Abbie stood at the crest of the hill, hands on her hips.

Alex barreled into the gazebo. "You yelled."

"I yelled the word *yes* to a proposal. I didn't yell for your help."

"Come on, bro, we are not needed here. Araceli, do you want us to leave Kyle's truck, or would you rather walk around the pond to the gate? Mandy is making breakfast."

"Walk."

Alex held out his hand to Kyle. "I'm really sorry about this morning."

"I think we are good. Imagine the story we will have to tell our grandkids about our engagement. Not everyone has to fight off a bodyguard to find out where his intended lives." Kyle's smile was genuine, but Araceli knew there had to be more to the story.

"He's a keeper. Not many guys even try to get a punch in. He managed three." Alex grinned.

"And I paid dearly for each one." Kyle touched the slight bruise on his cheek.

Abbie stepped into the gazebo, holding her phone. "Mandy says coffee cake and eggs are ready in forty minutes. Should she invite Candace and Zoe?"

"Yes. Now, will you two leave? I only have a few hours with this man before he has to drive a thousand more miles."

Abbie turned, but Alex stood there no matter how hard Araceli glared. "I have a couple days off. I could drive back with you, make sure you stay on the road, keep Araceli from worrying too much. You could drop me off at DFW, and I could hop a ride to O'Hare."

"Really?"

"Hey, after what you did to propose, the least I can do is make sure you live until the wedding."

"Thanks, man. Can you be ready by noon?"

"You bet." Alex ran up the hill after Abbie.

Araceli looked at her phone. "We have less than four hours. What do we need to do first?"

"This."

Kyle took Araceli in his arms and kissed her. "Celi, ma belle, *ou se solèy ki chofe mwen chak maten.*"

"What does that mean?"

"You are the sun that warms me in the morning. It's a Haitian endearment."

"Are there many of those?"

Kyle whispered against her lips. "A lifetime of them."

Epilogue

A ROOSTER CROWED SOMEWHERE. ARACELI cracked her eyelids. Darkness engulfed the room she shared with her husband.

Husband.

Mari.

The word was the same in French and Haitian Creole, and just thinking about it made her smile. He made her smile. The five weeks of her marriage had been heavenly. They'd honeymooned in Orlando for two weeks, then taken quick trips to Boston, Chicago, and Dallas before flying to Haiti.

After only a week, she had matched names with all the children, though they laughed at her mispronunciations and corrected her. Most of the children couldn't run faster than she could, but several of the boys challenged her to daily races down the dusty road in front of the orphanage. Yesterday, Tia had joined them and outrun them all. Haiti hadn't medaled in the Olympics since 1928. If she could find the right coach, and if it was something Tia really wanted, perhaps that could change. She'd promised Tia a short run this morning before breakfast. It would only be to the school and back and in the company of one of the gate guards and all the teen boys who thought they could keep up.

The rooster crowed again, but only moonlight peeked through the east window.

She rolled onto her side and reached for Kyle only to find she couldn't move.

The mosquito netting had trapped her. Again.

Hanging from a hoop attached to the ceiling, the netting had managed to tangle her up. This must be what a fly felt like in a spiderweb. Every move she made only pulled her cocoon tighter.

"Kyle? Kyle?"

He didn't move.

Araceli tugged on a section of the netting.

Crack.

The hoop and all the netting landed on the bed.

Kyle sat up. "Celi? Are you hurt?"

She couldn't stop laughing.

Kyle swam through the netting, trying to reach her.

"I'm s-sor-r-ry. I was just trying to k-kiss you-u." Laughter made it hard to speak.

"Kiss me or kill me?" The smile in his voice let her know he was teasing. Kyle continued to dig his way through the netting until his hand touched hers. "Found you."

"That is the only part of me I can move." Araceli wiggled her fingers.

"First thing in the morning, I'm purchasing a four-poster bed with hanging netting. I don't care if I have to import it from Paris and have it sent by private jet." He freed her arm.

"I am fairly sure they have them for sale in town."

"And here I hoped for a trip to Paris."

Araceli wriggled out of the rest of the cocoon. "You just wanted to get out of the interviews for Deah's Home for Trafficked Children. That place needs a better name."

Still under the mass of netting, Kyle pulled Araceli into his arms. "Now, about that kiss."

Araceli snuggled closer and leaned in. With only an inch separating their lips, a section of netting fell between them and brushed her lips. She sputtered.

Kyle laughed. "New bed first thing in the morning."

He moved the netting out of the way and kissed her passionately, then continued down her jaw line.

"Kyle, you should probably stop."

"Why?"

"Because it won't take much to get us tangled up in the netting again, and there are some things I don't want to explain to whoever answers our calls for help."

"That could be awkward." Kyle laughed. "First thing in the morning—new bed."

Araceli snuggled into his side. "That sounds like a very good idea."

Kyle kissed her once more, and they drifted back to sleep to the lullaby of a tropical rain beginning to fall outside the window

THE END

A person doesn't need to change the whole world,
just the world around them by being kind.

Mandy's Grandma Mae.

afterword

IN OCTOBER 2017, I ACCOMPANIED my longtime friends, Wendi and Evan Frederickson, on an assessment and repair trip to the Foyer de Sion orphanage in Haiti. Much of this book is based on my volunteer experience. Although we didn't paint the walls, our team did organize donations, which included dozens of rugby balls, and we rebuilt a kitchen. Two teen boys found me a battery-operated floor fan when I thought I just might melt, and dozens of children stole a piece of my heart.

The Queen Bees school I wrote about also exists, though under a longer Haitian name. However, Wendi does call them her "bees." Although I did not have an opportunity to visit there, I have heard and read many firsthand accounts of the valiant group of mothers who do everything they can to help to educate and feed their children. (Yes, they do raise chickens.).

A special thanks to Wendi Frederickson, schoolteacher, champion of children, and former board member of Foyer de Sion, for her help and insight with this book.

A portion of the profits of this book will be donated to help the children of Haiti.

acknowledgments

FOR OVER THIRTY YEARS I have been blessed to have a couple of brothers who are mine simply because they lived down the street and had no sisters. Evan and his wife Wendi have blessed my life in countless ways, not the least of which was the special trip to Haiti that inspired this book.

Tammy and Nanette are so willing to help make all my projects better and to read things so many times even in late night texts. I would never make it through a day without Sally and Cindy whose advice keeps me going. Thank you wonderful ladies. And to Araceli for letting me use her name.

Thanks also to Michele at Eschler Editing for the edits and finding oh so many little things to fix; any mistakes left in this book are not her fault. Nor are my excellent proofreaders to be blamed. Thank you ladies and gents!

My family, for sharing their home with the fictional characters who often got fed better than they did. And my husband who encourages me every crazy step of the way and puts up with all my messy spreadsheets.

And to my Father in Heaven for putting these wonderful people, and any I may have forgotten to mention, in my life. I am grateful for every experience and blessing I have been granted.

about the author

LORIN GRACE WAS BORN IN Colorado and has been moving around the country ever since, living in eight states and several imaginary worlds. She graduated from Brigham Young University with a degree in Graphic Design.

Currently she lives in northern Utah with her husband, four children, and a dog who is insanely jealous of her laptop. When not writing, Lorin enjoys creating graphics, visiting historical sites, museums, and reading.

Lorin is an active member of the League of Utah Writers and was awarded Honorable Mention in their 2016 creative writing contest short romance story category. Her debut novel, *Waking Lucy,* was awarded a 2017 Recommend Read award in the LUW Published book contest. In 2018 the first book in this series, Mending Fences with the Billionaire, also received a Recommend Read award.

You can learn more about her, and sign up for her writers club at loringrace.com or at Facebook: LorinGraceWriter